i write
HE DICTATES

REVENGE

Arnold Iwin Francis

BlueRose ONE.com
Stories Matter
NewDelhi • London

BLUEROSE PUBLISHERS
India | U.K.

BlueRose ONE.com
Stories Matter
NewDelhi • London

For permissions requests or inquiries regarding this publication, please contact:

BLUEROSE PUBLISHERS
www.BlueRoseONE.com
info@bluerosepublishers.com
+91 8882 898 898
+4407342408967

ISBN: 978-93-5989-136-1

Cover design: Rishav Rai
Typesetting: Rohit

First Edition: February 2024

PREFACE

How I wish I had a gun; I would have shot him-REVENGE.

"See how boisterous he gets?"

I really want to punch his nose and see red blood oozing out – REVENGE.

Is there one man amongst us, who wishes not to take Revenge - only the Saints.

Feel the surreptitious, macabre vendetta, the covert, furtive Revenge the Author, Arnold Iwin Francis presents in his flawless Novel.

Derrick Mitson

The taste of the last lickable chocolate you ate, still lingers in your mouth.

Some sizzling gossip you heard; you are all too eager to share with your mom.

The novel is stifling you with the wind, to keep the first page open for you to read.

Melody

Wish the Author, Arnold Iwin Francis, to take you on the road of Upheavals, placid and on the vendetta of this nauseating 'REVENGE' .

Can't believe it? Don't forget, it is the Serpentine Author, Arnold who draws Ink from the snake's fangs to write the inconceivable.

June and Desmond

I Thought I knew my friend, Arnold, very well but I was in for a surprise. He could wield his fists very well but when he wielded the pen to bring the alphabets into submission and placed the novel in my hands, I was taken up completely by surprise. When I read it, I felt the same what he himself feels- The elves must have written it in the night.

Shashi and Sudhir Chowdhry

CONTENTS

1

WHAT AN INCIDENT!

"Yahoooooo, yeah-ah-ah "he shouted till it rang out and pierced the ear-drums. Usually this road was never congested (over-flowing with people) but certainly there were few people pressing the aching shoulders of the road anytime of the day and night. Today it was surprisingly empty. Shawn, the king was coming and he even balanced the scooty for 1-2 seconds while both his hands were flailing up in the air. He turned the bend and like a looming monster a truck, with a singing sardar "Mera rang de basanti chola" screeched and swerved out of his way, only to brush him and carried on, feeling everything was okay in his inebriated (drunk) condition or did he avoid the imbroglio (confusion) the police creates for them. "Wham, thud, thud" went the scooty grazing and caressing past the side of the truck and leaving silver marks- the colour of the two-wheeler. "Mummeee---------ee" was loud and shrill in the air as Shawn was thrown like a shuttle-cock with a thud on a patch of green grass on the edge of the road. The 'seven sisters (birds) were the only mute spectators who may have witnessed the whole scene with their usual cacophony of noise and cackle and hopped further away unconcerned, to feed on the delicacies the good earth had provided them. Shawn lay motionless, as they came to know his name later.

There was no doctor or anyone else to declare if he still had a pulse. This was a confirmatory test that all accidents occur on curves. The road still ran as though there were legs under it and its face was jet-black, as black as tar-coal, for it was an accomplice in such a shameful accident.

A car whizzed past without noticing the sleeping scooty at one side of the road from the hard kisses of the truck where the paint had peeled with dents. Perhaps the driver was dozing or purposely eyes closed with and trepidation of the numerous visits to the police-stations and the rough and callous treatment meted out to them.

Two innocent boys Trilok ladla and Aftab on a motor-cycle, one driving furiously and the other standing at the back with arms akimbo shouting hoarsely 'Yahooooooooo' and were gone.

"Stop, stop" the one at the back shouted to his friend who was driving. The motor-cycle screeched with pain at the sudden jamming of the brakes and the heat generated due to the friction between the tyres and the road. When friends, thick as thieves, (very close) turn enemies even all the thawed(melted) ice on the Antarctica cannot cool them.

"Now, what's wrong?" shouted the one driving.

“Didn’t you see a scooty on the road, “half panting as though he had been running and not his ‘Dhup-dhup’ (Motor-cycle).

Boys will be boys. In a jiffy, the motor-cycle had turned direction and was gulping the road ferociously.

“Stop, stop can’t you see?” as the pillion rider jumped off the bike. Both scrutinized the silver scooty and were more than eager to help and then it struck them. Their eyes roved 360 degrees and what should have been apparent (clear) in the first instant struck like a thunder-bolt. In the soft green grass, holding like a baby, lay strewn a motionless body.

“Don’t touch, it will be a police case”, admonished the driver but his friend was of a different temperament and did not bother about consequences. He had seen his doctor uncle from Germany handle almost a similar case in the biting cold in the wee hours (early) of the morning. His uncle had gone to the police –station and shook up the sleeping inspector at his desk, told him to carry the man, who was alive but could die with delay, to a hospital in his jeep. The sleep-soaked inspector wanted to first do paper-work but his uncle presented his identity card and took all responsibility on himself. The inspector had no choice. “See the value Indian –born German doctor had for human life? The man still lives and eternally grateful to his uncle.”

With grit and determination and trembling hands, he caught the muscular hands of this motion-less strange and like his doctor uncle gave it a hard twitch. There was a moaning sound and then everything was quiet.

Trilok, trying to thwart (stop) him from playing with fire was left with no option but to comply. They raced him to the nearest hospital where the doctors refused to attend for police had to be called first. Just before the khakhi uniform (police) arrived and with a lot of cajoling the doctor administered some injections that should and would revive him. The concussion on the head was not very severe- the soft grass, where he had landed due to the accident, had played mother and secured him from fatal harm. Few bruises here and there, were the tell-tales that would remain.

An hour passed but his eyes were shut tight. Both the friends prayed for him to regain consciousness and their prayers were answered with the arrival of the police and trouble.

"Oh, Charlie, what's your name?" How rude can they be? Didn't their mother ever teach them manners?" But when they spoke only "my name sir" was audible.

"Who else, you fiend?" shouted the inspector in his hoarse voice. "Sir" in his most humble voice which could hardly be heard stammered Aftab. Now he realized the gravity of the situation and his friend's words not to meddle and come in the cross-hairs of the police.

The inspector suddenly lunged forward, caught him by his side-burns and shook him up like a rag doll. "So, you have been having fun with your friends and landed him in this trouble?"

"No,no,no sir, I do---------------------" and then he was too petrified(scared) for his lips to open." I know this is some girl's chakkar, come to the police-station and I'll skin you to get the truth out of you "roared the man in khakhi.

Both shriveled into their cocoon further, unable to utter a word. For the first time since the incident Trilok's thoughts secretly ran to his father and mother. My dear boys and girls it is always in trouble that you remember your parents- maybe that is the reason why God has given us these two very special people to pour our troubles to. Trilok's dad had repeatedly told him not to ever get into the clutches of the police and he had vehemently argued with him. Today he had lost his tongue and whatever little he could muster to say was incoherent (not clear) in front of the fusillade of his fetid (unpleasant smell) questions. His ill-conceived and gory story could only draw flak and an inane (silly) grin.

"Sir" his friend timidly stammered. "You brat, your chance" thundered the inspector." You don't listen with kindness" and caught a tuft of Aftab's hair till it came out with its roots, in his filthy, toad-skinned hand. Both Friends looked at each other in dismay and then their eyes fell on the accident victim's face which twitched slightly and was quiet again. So, there was hope and he wanted to shout, only the stare of the man in uniform, as though he would decimate (finish) them, froze the lips and sealed it with an Aligarh lock. Friends looked furtively (secretly) at each other's trousers to see if they were wet. Both had acquired an Achilles' heel to ward off such an evil design by this unscrupulous man.

The hospital was bustling with patients, as is usual in India, so there was no room in the I.C.U. "Sister Margaret how is the patient? "inquired the doctor as he entered after seeing the other sick people.

"We have put him on the drip but he needs a bed in the ICU". She spoke in her South Indian twang which was both visible and audible when she pronounced 'yellow' as 'ellow'. One country but what different tongues. You can discern (make out) a person from Punjab with their accent. Uttar Pradesh people don't say 'mai ' (I) but say 'Hum' (We). The Nawabi tongue of Lucknow is extremely sweet and music to the ears. Their 'aap' is known the world over for they never use the word 'Tu'. (You). 'Mahro Rajasthan' (My Rajasthan) is a little split of the Hindi word 'Mera Rajasthan'. 'Tusi ki gal hai' is a lively Punjabi talk and our film industry has utilized the language to such an extent that they merge into Hindi and Hindi into Punjabi without much fanfare. 'Hami aaschi' is spoken so sweetly that everyone believes

Bengalis speak with a rasgulla (sweet) in their mouths.

2

WHAT A RELIEF!

The nurse took the doctor aside and whispered in his ears "Doctor, the inspector is beating the boys in the hospital."

"For what?" jumped the doctor as though he got an electric shock.

Kind of the inspector to just pull the collar of Aftab and Trilok and to connect on the mobile to their fathers. "Hey son of a gun what does your father do?" the inspector asked brusquely. (rudely)

"Sir,sa, sa,sa-----------------" Sir refused to come out from the cavity of the mouth of the two boys. They were now shivering in their pants. This was the last thing they wanted their parents to hear. Why was God not helping them? Had he become deaf, dumb or was it HIS pass-time to enjoy the sufferings of innocent humans. These thoughts passed their heads without a sound. Was it the silent movie era of Charlie Chaplin?

"Inspector, what are you doing to the boys?" came the pleasant voice of the smiling doctor.

"I'm doing my duty to get the truth out of these rascals," retorted the inspector with a smile that refused to come out of his impenetrable cheeks. Maybe, with all the murders, burglary cases and hardened criminals they become hard like a coconut shell and even the inside, the human part takes on the hue (color) of the top. Only with their immediate family they are soft, but that is human psychology which is an integral part of any individual character. Imagine this heinous murderer from Ghaziabad who was very much in the news recently, who killed people with his whims and fancies at the drop of a hat, could not stay in solitary confinement. The judge had to revoke the order so that he could lead a normal life. Just imagine at one side he killed people and on the other he could not stay alone. Many a times I have sat thinking of Charles Dickens writing of solitary confinement given to British convicts, thrown in the confines of Australia and how they must have suffered. Man by nature is very hard-hearted only with their immediate kin it is a different story. Isn't the world one big family – some living close, some living far. Let a natural calamity strike, like an earth-quake of 9 and above on the Richter scale (10 is the highest for people who are unaware) or a tsunami of unprecedented scale which wipes out a majority of us and see how we run to save the rest. In times of peace can't we stay peaceful, instead of deploying armies to wipe out the other country from the face of the earth. Some will call it idle gossip and skip reading this paragraph.

Wonderful, my man, go seek disaster for yourself! Japan is a wonderful example with people of Hiroshima and Nagasaki still carrying wounds of the war and their pledge for cessation of war. If, time and again, on celluloid we are shown the atrocities and pangs of war, people will take a hatred for it and love will reign the world and happiness will pour from all directions. Just ask yourself

"where are we heading and what do we want from life?"

"Please inspector, they have brought an accident victim to save him. He has had a concussion and it is my duty to see that you don't harass them. Till the victim gets okay you will have to wait," said the doctor in his soothing but authoritative voice. Both the boys simply adored him and both dwelt on the same subject whether anybody born in this world could ever hate him. Why God never created a world which had people who only understood Love and never knew what hate was? Didn't HE know this was bound to happen and the only outcome of leaving the people free? And yet without HIS wish not a leaf would stir. It does make us sad, to think, SOMEONE was playing with our lives. How else do you explain the poverty and sufferings of the poor and the rich getting richer.

An angel, in the form of this doctor, had descended from Heaven. Was it the handiwork of the ALMIGHTY to pull this string and then that?

Just one minute back they were burning in the fires of Hell and now the world looked so rosy. Which Rosy did these two boys know that they were talking about or was it the rose flower with it's lovely aroma? Whichever you choose, you are bound to get thorns with it but boys can't resist the two. Marry in a hurry and regret at leisure. For the first time, since they met the accident victim, did their thoughts linger onto their first day in college and what friends they would have made especially the fairer sex. Their mothers would have been very eager to know what'll friends they made and would have nudged-nudged them till some girl's name fell out of their secretive tongues, closely guarded by the mouth that refused to open.

"How can we thank you doctor for saving us from this men(ace)?" The 'ace' just sat on the tip of the tongue and was too scared to leave and was as silent as a 'p' in pneumonia (pronounced as ne-mo-nia). The lips seemed to be getting their freedom but stopped short seeing the cadaverous look (sick look) of the boisterous inspector. The inspector donned (wore) his beret, straightened his uniform till the crease of his smart attire(clothes) fell in place, like the boys he tortured to keep them straight or was like a trained soldier.

"I'll see you two, too soon for you to believe," he retorted in his cacophonous (unpleasant) voice, which few people, er sorry, no one would ever want to hear in their life-time. He waved a good-bye to the doctor and vanished on his motor-bike, as though it had wings.

"Remember, these are the same policemen who secure the safety of our families. Your mom and dad, your brothers and sisters roam freely, without fear of any trouble-makers. There would be utter, unruly chaos without these khakhi uniforms roaming on the roads, keeping an eagle-eye on the bad elements in the day and an owl's night vision to keep a vigil in the darkness of the night and to penetrate the opaqueness (darkness) with a piercing eye and a very, very brave heart- a heart ready to burst but not budge at the provocation of these misguided youths," sighed the smiling lips of the smiling doctor, "and thank you for being so brave as to bring the accident victim who is in such a precarious (dangerous) state, but with your prayers and the nurse's care, God cures and heals." Such a modest doctor was difficult to find who never mentioned the prescriptions he wrote for all the patients. Both the boys wondered, when had they prayed and when did the doctor overhear them?

3

What Is Blood

The flimsy silence was shattered by a very familiar wail of crying, when the door burst open with Trilok`s mother in sight and the father following at a distance with a grim face.

"Where is my son and where has he got hurt?" the mother cried loud beating her chest as though she was addressing the world as an audience. Had she been in any political party, all the votes would have fallen in her lap with her impassioned cry. Aftab wanted to laugh out loud, while his friend, Trilok, almost choked the smile on his quizzical face, to see his mother in such a sad state when he was fit as a fiddle but seeing the gravity of the situation just caught and clasped his mother. All along the way she was besieged (seized) with the thought that her son was carried on the stretcher to the hospital operating table and doctors pouring over him stitching and clipping his tattered and torn blood-stained body. A host of pain and suffering had been strewn in front of her and had taken an insurmountable hue like mountain Kilimanjaro in Africa standing facing you in the eye.

Gossip and rumour, very seldom escapes the ladies even if the truth stands in front.

"Get out of your reverie" shouted the father and shook the mother, "our son is hale and hearty and thank you GOD for it." The mother slowly absorbed the situation as though she was a blotting paper and then the truth dawned on her. Both father and mother were besides themselves with joy and glee as though they had won the first prize of Maharashtra state lottery. No son would ever know how much he is treasured by his mother and father till he himself becomes a father and then most of the times it is too late for he sees an empty chair, where his father sat.

By now the nurses had shifted the accident victim into the next door ICU (Intensive care unit) and was visible partially from the ¾ th translucent and $1/4^{th}$ plain glass. Why it was so, we were not there to decide and then it was none of our business or were we in the detective business? Trilok and Aftab looked very secure, now that their parents had arrived and they felt an ethereal happiness descending on them for saving the victim's life by bringing him to the hospital. Now they felt the urge to know what his name was? Where did he live? Who were his parents? Did he have other brothers and sisters, especially sisters and if they stood a chance? Secretly, in their mind's eye, unknown to each other, they were in chariots with his sister in their arms.

They just closed their eyes and refused to open for fear the truth may dawn with a very different ending and then only a foolish guy would want such a lovely dream curtailed. Half-awake they refused to let the dream go by. Half an hour went by in such blissful thinking. Trilok's father, who had been restraining the mother from waking the two, felt it was time to do so. He tried to call them softly but they shut their eyes tighter. He gave up the half-hearted attempt. The mother came on the scene – tried to call them, tried to even shake them lightly but to no avail. She tried once again and then got panicky, thinking about all the rumours that normally solidifies in a lady's head and more in a mother's. She started believing something amiss and without thinking further picked a small bucket of water, just brought in by an old couple, and emptied it on top of their heads. The dreams just got washed away. Both friends jumped up and in so doing banged their heads hard enough for hillock like swellings to appear on their heads. It looked more like a blue-black frog on each head between the tufts of hair and ready to hop. Instead of helping them, there was such a peal of laughter from everyone present and the loudest was from the father and mother.

What if the boy did not survive? This question did not even trespass their minds for it could become a police case and they would be the first suspects in the accident. This trauma did not cross their minds for their mother and father were with them. No place on this planet can be more secure than with the ones who gave you birth.

When it rains, it pours. Today every word of it was true. A Keralite nurse in impeccable (perfect) white uniform, with sunken eyes, as though she had not slept for days, came running out of the ICU with a forced smile rubbed on her face with good news. "He has opened his eyes but still in a daze and even his speech is incoherent (not clear) and inaudible (can't be heard) and has a slur, as her eyes searched and cornered the two boys. "Sister can we go in and see him?" both the boys in one voice screamed. Both were already pulling their collar up feeling they would be felicitated as heroes on the first day of their college lives, without attending any class. You may have to wait and even the inspector will be called to take his statement," as she walked away.

Hearing the word 'inspector' a chill ran down their spine, as though the chill was a rat. All this time, the mother and father just stood hearing the 'going ons' and elated (happy) at the deed of their children and happier that they were unharmed.

There was another outburst outside and a fusillade of inconsolable weeping with tears streaming down the cheeks in a torrential 'train' of salt water. The water runs out to cool the brain and the salt that is true to the person joins in, forming the so called 'tears'. This is not the doctor's view but foolish people like us, who like to tickle the funny bone and make the very serious person smile, if not laugh. Foolish indeed but sometimes it works. Tears and smiles are just part and parcel of a hospital.

4

WE TREAT DOCTORS LIKE GODS

"Doctor is this your nature or you force yourself and talk with everyone in such a loving tone?" Queried Aftab.

"Oh! Do I? Then I certainly deserve a pat "and with his right hand actually patted his Left shoulder. "My two children, a girl and a boy, will be very proud to hear their father being praised. They always say 'my father is the best' but every night I have to tell them a joke and then how many jokes can I remember? Trilok immediately butted in and told the doctor to tell his children this joke which he had heard two days back. "New admissions were going on in the school. A father was filling the admission form for his child. When he reached the column- mother tongue? He wrote – long and a berating tongue and fit to be cut off". The doctor just doubled up with laughter. "My children will be very happy tonight but right now I have to go and see other patients Besides being brave, you have a lovely sense of humour. You are students, I believe, what are you studying?" Both boys in one accord shouted "Architecture" and also proudly named their college. "Wow! I'm proud of that and before I rush to see my patients what I remember of school days I'll tell if I still remember correctly.

The mistake of a pathologist leads the physician in the lurch, that of an architect under the debris but that of a school reflected in the nation "and finishing that the doctor just vanished inside the hospital. Childhood memories made a Bee -line as Shawn lay on the hospital bed, which had kicked out many patients so that they could stand on their feet and happiness.

5

Childhood Comes Just Once

Mrs. Sheila Singh alights from the rickshaw when her son, Shawn, from the door-way of his house runs to meet her. "Shawn I told you to play with the neighbour's son. Where is he and why are you alone?" "Mamma, aunty told us to play outside, because someone has come to see Niti didi but from outside I heard them asking for Niti didi's hand in marriage. Mamma the boy will get married only to the hand. What about the other parts of the body?"

Mrs. Sheila Singh - "Beta you get married only to the hand but the rest of the body comes free with it. Just like you buy a detergent soap and you get another one free. (Mrs Sheila smiles). "Phew, its lovely inside and blistering hot in the sun outside "the petulant and pouting lips of Mrs. Sheila Singh screeched. There was no answer except the air-conditioner talking to the fan in whispers inaudible to the human ear -"I keep my head and the room cool though my back-side is on fire." Poor fan- "You just do not know my condition; I'm hanging, rotating day and night by my neck, just for a wisp of air. I'm giddy over it (air) but it keeps running away from me."

Children do not feel the scorching heat of the sun in summers or the bone chilling winds that blow in the north of India where temperatures fluctuate from 0 degrees Celsius to 45 degrees Celsius.

Holding each other's ears in a circle were five children playing `Aala bala makri ka jala ` {spider's web}. In another corner were a little bigger children who had got the breeze of the public schools and wanted to show-off with their prowess at English, were playing in a bigger circle of boys and girls `I sent a letter to my moother {mother} on the way I drapped {dropped} it, some natty {naughty} boy must have picked it up and put it in his focket, {pocket}. Is that you? Is that you? ` And yet in the big field were boys playing cricket drenched to the skin. It's the poor ball which should be in the cool I.C.U. for being beaten up so badly and then put to shame when hit for a sixer by the whole crowd in the stadium which goes berserk at the precarious condition of the ball whose intestines, liver, heart all protrude out of it's thick skin.

One six year old boy among all these children to another seven year's old- "Tell me yaar {friend} does the sun have a father who does not know the spelling of `son` that he spells it as `sun`?"

The other boy- "I think the Sun is a Very big torch which it switches off in the night for us to sleep".

The sun shone with all it's fury right through the year; it was the good mother Earth which maintained it's distance from it, going in an elliptical path to cover it's revolution around the Sun in 365 days. The places which fight with their mother Earth to get the warmth of the Sun from it's 93 million miles away source, are also doused with the blisters of the scalding hot rays of the Sun which takes some 7-8 minutes to flood us with light and heat. The rays come with good intentions to help mankind as friends and to alleviate the darkness of the night; too much of anything creates problems for us and in this case it leaves blisters on too much exposure but in the normal course it gives vitamin D, very much needed for the calcium of our bones. That is why someone has rightly adjudged "better a little fire that warms than a big one that burns".

"Don't you know the festival of colours, Holi, is at hand when the shivering cold recedes, giving way to this inviting warmth" chanted his mother in her sweet, lilting voice. "Very soon, children with their pretty, some dirty, little feet from around the colony and neighborhood will trudge the roads and come knocking on doors with 'Tesus' hand-crafted with their mother's help. They recite funny words that are very pleasing to the ears."

Earlier, it was the tu,tu, tu, tu, with breath held to play kabbaddi. Then came the silent era of Charlie Chaplin with black and white television and as technology grew the Eastman colour and the Technicolour and today an abyss of entertainment at our finger-tips.

Chirpy as Shawn was and excited about almost anything "What is this Tesu?" with palatable excitement that you could read on his face and the mother's face puffing up with pride like a puffer fish when thrown by the angler in disgust on the ground without a drop of water.

"It is like a palanquin (Doli) that a new bride in some remote village come to their new home in. Only a Tesu is small, two feet and maybe made of card-board and a little mud. Four to six pretty hands carry the structure lovingly for some idols of Gods are placed on it. They stop at houses they know or feel they will be welcome and pours the magma they have been accumulating for the full year in the form of words and gushes out like lava from a volcano" chanted the mother in her benign (kind and gentle) voice.

Shawn sat on the sofa, facing the door, which sank down with even his meagre weight. His eyes were glued to the road outside, little realizing that it was still afternoon.

The dahlias in the garden that were standing upright, smiling and sending whiffs of their aroma at every passerby in the morning, now stood with their heads drooping, slightly wilted, as though a newly-wed bride, shy and demure, stood facing her groom for the first time with her head down. The sweet-peas in their glittering colours clung onto the twine but with the slightest breeze went scampering to catch on to the thread at the first opportunity. The larkspurs in their red, white and purple colours kept swaying in the wind that had lost all velocity and hence inviting a gentle breeze.

The larks (Birds)for they too were happy as a lark. The pansies had the king and queen seated in the middle with purple, yellow hues thrown in abundance that only a throne could be adorned with. The humming-bird like a helicopter stood still in the air with their long beaks sucking the nectar that the flowers offered to the guests with pride and with a smile like most of us Indians do. 'The ornaments of this house are the friends who frequent it'. The snap-dragon (Dog flower as some people prefer to call) had wilted not from the heat of the sun but from some naughty hands of the children. They still smiled courageously, happy that they could snap like a dog with a slight twist of the children's fingers.

Without a word his mother had softly tapped him, as only a mother can. So he had slept on the sofa and all the lovely flowers were part of his dreams.

Every night we lumber in our slumber. Some dream that they have knocked a tiger flat with their bare hands. others have taken on ten goons who were troubling the girls on the train and yet there were others who draw less than a few hundred per month and find it difficult to make two ends meet in real life but dream they are drawing millions per annum. Let them dream and be happy.

The knuckles of Shawn's hands tried to rub the sleep off his eyes as though they were two erasers, "mamma, the tesus must have gone, why didn't you wake me?" "Don't worry my dahling, no tesus have passed as yet" chimed his mother, as she pulled him to her bosom to savour his closeness and he her warmth and security that every child needs in this world.

Afternoon turned to evening; evening turned to night but no trace of the tesus. Some children did pass the door on their own errands but no sign of the elusive tesu, much to the chagrin of Shawn. "Don't worry my baby, it will come", soothed his mother, hoping she was not wrong in her judgement.

Tick-tock, tick-tock went the clock. The seconds needle, long and slim, traversing a full circle in it's pre-determined time of sixty seconds with exact precision. The short, stout old lady-like handle moved slowly in sudden spurts declaring it's hours with a sweet, melodious chime. seconds to seconds, the second-hand needle, coloured red, moved as though it was just oiled and slipped past all hurdles effortlessly as though it was brand new. It was. Just a small punch of a joke for your poky nose.

"Mamma, why is time standing still?" precocious child that Shawn was.

"Beta, time is running as usual with Hussein Bolt's speed, only your anxiety is running at a fierce rate." "Mamma, one day daddy was telling me I'm a nut. *Is this the same nut and bolt you are talking of? "Beta, as you grow older you will understand? Have patience and by the way, Usain Bolt is the fastest runner in the world."*

There was a commotion at the door and Shawn burst his lungs with' Tesu' and sure enough it was. Four children put the tesu down and waited for someone from the house to come and pamper them with requests and money. Shawn nearly knocked the chair on his way as he sprinted towards the door. Besides the four children, there was a tail of at least 7-8 urchins and on-lookers.

Audience ready, the children did not miss the chance. With one accord, they forayed with a fusillade of words, never heard before.

" Mera Tesu yahi gare
Khane ko mange dahi-bara
Dahi –bara may mirche bahut
Aage dekhu kanji hauz
Kanji hauz may char ghari
Charo may zanzeer pari
Jab ghanta ghar bajta tha
Chalta musafir hasta tha
Hasta tha bhai badharak
Aage dekho nai sarak
Nai sarak may boya bajra
Aage dekho Sha-shadra
Sha-shahdra may lag gayi aag
Aage dekho Ghaziabad
Ghaziabad ki oonchia tari
Nai ne mari phenk katari
Nai bay naike, yeh kya kaam
Ghar bheteh hai, hay jajmaan."

Many nearby houses had opened their doors to hear this rhapsody but now quietly closed the doors for fear they will have to delve deep into their pockets and share some hard earned coins with the children. The clinking coins brought a smile on the children's faces as they moved on.

A baby is born with clenched(closed) fist so that the dollars, euros, francs of America and Europe; dirham of Dubai, baht of Thailand and ringette of Malaysia and of course rupees of our beloved India do not fly off. This insatiable (that cannot be satisfied) thirst continues for life; those who can shake this habit off become almost like Gods on Earth and those who cannot, become humans. This craving for this lush-green, even soiled notes brings a sheen to the rich, which the poor cannot penetrate and look at them in awe. There are murders, endless strife, corruption to get into other peoples' shoes, little knowing there are millions waiting to get into their cozy shoes. Just see the fun when size 7 tries to get into a shoe meant for size 5- he squirms into the shoe half inside and half outside and the gait he develops is no better than a drunkards and the awkward sight is worth watching to bring laughter to your face.

6

Why No One Told Me That Childhood Days Are The Best.

Hardly had the children gone, when there was a light tap at the door. Mum opened the door to a handsome young man. Shawn screamed "daddy" and clung to his father like he would never leave him again. The father kissed him, kissed him like a doting father and gave a peck on the mother's cheek. Shawn wobbled on his legs forward and hung onto his legs who picked him along in his left arm and planted kisses till a tree of kisses grew. Now please don't ask me for the name of this tree but as soon as scientists find a name I'll let you into the secret- till then put a forced smile and read on.

" Yeah, it's been a lovely day but nothing like being home" chuckled Anuj Singh to his darling wife, Sheila. Their eyes met and you could see the love oozing out of them. All the weariness of the journey just vanished in that instant, such is the happiness of a home, knitted and crafted by the lady of the house. This is the only way a house turns into a home.

Daddy picked up a small plastic bag which he had dropped on the ground while lifting his life's treasure, his son. From the bag he pulled out a lovely car. "A car for my lovely son and a scarlet red lip-stick for the mother. Wasn't this the colour you were searching for in the market?" The mother twitched her nostrils with a little shake of her head in accent. Shawn was already testing the lip-stick on his mother's lips. "Doesn't mamma look pretty, dad?" "Whoa, but not prettier than my pet, Shawn". "Why not, after all he's your son? As you always say we women are just soil in the garden and you the gardener who grows the seeds." "I love to trouble you but you know I don't mean a thing, "smiled her very loving husband.

I wonder with who God plays foot-ball and what a kick? The Sun (foot-ball) goes traversing half the Earth, smiling as it goes with the cheering crowd, down on the earth. A second kick for the second hemisphere of the earth and the full day is done. When the Sun is in the other hemisphere the moon with it's feeble moon-light comes dancing in inviting couples in love to hold hands while it keeps the piercing eyes of the parents away. Then who could be playing cricket for many of the shooting stars come crashing down to earth like cricket balls going for a sixer.

7

Wonderful Days – College Days

This mother's small baby, Shawn, was amidst the stars, the moon and the Sun till one day he could read all about them and understand. Today he was to go to college –his very first day.

Endless days had gone in Shawn's selection to the eminent college where most of India dreams of going but these youngsters don't even get to see the gates leading to it. Admission forms had to be filled on-line. It was the computer age and anyone not computer savvy was not fit for almost anything related to the advances of science. Fortunately, Shawn was computer savvy and did not have to take rounds of cyber cafes. Instead, he devoted time in sipping coffee along with his beloved mother. It was such a lovely time to be together with his dear ones, only dad was away on business, as usual. "Mum, I feel I'm frolicking and gamboling (run happily) on the green meadows like a lamb with her mother in close vicinity and feeling very safe." "You look more like a charged bull with the dirty face that you carry around." Mother was pulling her son's legs. Shawn must check if his left leg has grown longer than his right one due to this leg pulling. Ha, haa. Hundreds and thousands of mothers, who are on this page, will realize they have done exactly what this mother is doing in this book and relating it to them. Life is not so different for one mother to another.

"Mum, it's already 7.15a.m. and first day in college I have Orientation classes which is a must for every fresher. It gives you an insight into which direction you are heading."" Break-fast is ready, my dahling, and the chair is waiting to caress and pamper your bottom with it's softness." Shawn sat down with a thump and the chair creaked with displeasure but no sound came for it was too sturdy. Shawn looked at the cheese, the golden crisp aloo-parantha (potato) and the fried egg with a yearning which turned to disdain at the mere thought of increasing the circumference of his belly. "Mum why do you tempt me with such delicacies? Do better things than to squander your time on cooking." He picked up the glass of cold milk and gulped it down his throat. Unusual for him, for normally he would slowly sip, turning the glass round and round and comparing it with the previous level, so that he would know how much he was taking in one gulp and then drink slow or fast depending on the time available. Other times, he would sit for break-fast as though he was on a fast for long and would finish every vestige of food till the table looked empty. In the night, before sleeping, mother and sometimes father would tease him " No more break-fast till morning" and all would have a hearty laugh. One night, Shawn's dad came up with this teaser and even the mother was baffled. Why were the soldiers tired on the 1st of April?" Both Shawn and the mother wrecked their brains for a good quarter of an hour but arrived at no good answer till the father came to their rescue –The soldiers were tired on the 1st of April because they just had a March of 31 days.

Shawn would guzzle everything down and yet was sinewy and muscular. He was also turning out to be very handsome- genes of the father, mother played a very big part, but here in this case there was not the slightest trace of the mother's traits. Even outsiders would point out whether the mother had any part to play in his birth and poor mother would only blush and keep quiet. The father would console her that gossip-mongers loved to hurt anyone.

As much as Shawn wished for the needles of the clock not to budge they had taken wings and like a cheetah ran at 100 km per hour. The clock smiled but could not trespass to strike the eight gongs for it was 7.30 a.m. Fifteen precious minutes had elapsed raising Shawn's anxiety to reach the premises of his college.

"Bye-mom" and rained kisses on her oval, rosy cheeks. Father was on his usual business trips to earn for his lovely family. He and his family had everything that God could bestow. My India is a wonderful country where it seems there are more holidays than are school-days but recently I came to know, even Australia, has 8 to 10 weeks of study and then 2 weeks of holidays. Our India is absolutely secular with a rainbow of religions adorning it and all demanding holidays for their numerous festivals. Patience is the mother of virtue and India has loads of it intact. I cannot help but take my hat off and my chest swells up with pride.

With a heart pounding, Shawn pressed the ignition of his mum's scooty which purred to life. It was not sweltering heat till now, being early morning, but she did not canter, trot (horse's speed) but galloped like a horse. His scooty was jumping as his heart was thumping.

Happy as a lark, he zipped through the road, all too eager to reach the college which was not much of a distance. He was drenched with happiness at the mere thought of making and meeting new friends.

8

WHERE IS SHAWN?

It was almost fifty minutes past the college time for Shawn to arrive home, but there was no sign of him. The anxiety filled mother's eyes were spread like a red carpet for the arrival back of her son from the college.She gave another half an hour, thinking he may be busy making friends with new boys and girls but still the gate did not make any rattling sound while opening nor did the latch sing it's usual music while opening and closing. She felt annoyed with her son that he did not care that his mother was waiting for him. Then a slight panic arrived in her brains like an earthquake of 7.3 on the Richter scale and shook her. She phoned everyone from the directory in the locality but their children had already arrived. Then she shuffled Shawn's papers for the college's number.

"Could I please know if Shawn Singh of Architecture 1st year came for classes in your college today? I'm his mother.

"How come ma'am you are his mother and don't know whether your son came to college or not? Please ma'am we do not entertain such queries but give us fifteen minutes to verify," came the sweet voice of the receptionist.

It was not even ten minutes when the mobile lying stretched out on the table, looking defunct and dead, rang out loud and clear, springing to life in the deafening silence of her reverie to wake her up with a jolt from her thoughts. "Yes please, I'm Shawn Singh's mother," in a very subdued voice. The thought that the college could respond so fast did not even strike her but it spoke volumes about the efficacy of the technological advances the prestigious college had made. Maybe, at sombre times she would realize.

"Ma'am, Shawn Singh of 1st year Architecture has not attended the first day of college and the Director, I'm sure, will take a very serious view of it. He had granted two days, on your husband's request, to your son to come from home for this is a completely residential institute "and hung up.

"But how can that be? He went in the morning and what will his father think? Did the air around him swallow him up? Does he have way-word friends, with who he went away? He was so keen to go to college?" Then she realized the futility of it for the mobile was dead. Such a harsh word at such a juncture brought tears to her eyes, as though it was a well of salt-water.

All her five senses became numb and the sixth one just hovered over her head like a twinkling star, one second here and the second second it just vanished. Her joy of sending her son in the morning to college was turning to despair now. She shook herself but nothing untoward happened. She shook again and a vague and faint figure seemed to appear but she could not discern who it was. She walked out of the house, not knowing what to do dressed as she was in her home clothes.

"Hullo, how is your husband? I have not seen him for almost a week, "a smiling, pleasant face of a neighbour appeared, whose voice blended the sound of shrillness, hammered flat and he had a virile funny bone ready at the sight of any human with an appropriate humour. He realized this was no moment to miss his joke but before he could crack one, she had disappeared. The poor neighbour was left in the lurch but he was such a happy-go-lucky man –"Next time------------------"

Mrs. Singh dialed her husband and told him "Hurry Home". "Hari Om" the husband repeated finding it very funny. Fortunately, he re-dialed her number to verify and was shocked to hear about Shawn. He whispered something in his friend's ear and left hurriedly for home. He found his wife waiting at the gate of their house and she hopped into the car. Was she a rabbit that she hopped?

He drove straight to the Sadar Bazar police-station, after his wife told him about their son, Shawn. He lodged a complaint there about his missing son. They were in the dark about Shawn's whereabouts. How come police are always in the dark even in broad day-light? Imagine the police, solve jig-saw puzzles at their job and earn their livelihood. The foot-baller plays with a foot-ball to rise to fame. Only the poor scientist, engineer and doctor has to wreck their brains for a living. Even the politician does not have to be learned enough but must be suave and eloquent in his talk and know the art of folding his/her hands in a dignified 'Namaste' and he has played safe with the majority of votes in his lap.

It was a clear case of communication gap between police-stations otherwise this riddle would have been a solved puzzle. Ofcourse, the Station house Officer had asked them for Shawn's photograph which they did not carry but would supply soon.

The car was the only solace which cuddled them in their seats and the four wheels soothingly and fast took them to the desired destination, the prestigious college of India. Everyone was there, at their beck and call, to help. They got addresses and phone numbers of students who were in 1st year of Architecture. The first was a girl who had no idea of Shawn. The second mobile showed 'busy'. The third was also very vague but his friend, who was not from the college, nudged him about some accident he had heard about this morning. "We cannot pin-point, but this is all we heard this morning." "Thank you, my son" which was more a cry than the usual chirpy, clever father of Shawn and hung up. Mother and father were playing detectives unknowingly to find their son but with a lot of uneasiness and stress, that the Australians are so fond of talking.

The search for doctor's clinics, nursing homes started in right earnest. Everywhere they went, they drew a blank. Mirori Pal hospital had many accident cases but none to fit Shawn's description, besides most of them were above 40-45 years old. Anyway, all was not futile for they got phone numbers of lot of hospitals etc. Their voices had turned hoarse from calling and any outsider would have felt the usual tiff between husband and wife had led to it. Even in other peoples' miseries, some keep themselves amused this way. I feel very sorry for people who don't enter into wedlock and miss the whiff of their wife's tongue, worse than that of a cobra snake, especially if you have shaken her maiden name's tree, dropping leaves that unfold linen washed in public- God save you.

If you are a diplomatic husband and raise the banner of the wife's side in praise, you can etch and carve that date on your brain to register the happiest day of your life. I have come to the conclusion that all the diplomats in the world are the off-springs of the endeavours of so many wives who have worked hard in creating this specialized institute of diplomacy.

When Mr. Singh phoned the biggest hospital 'Cuppolo' the description suited their son, Shawn. What a relief and yet uneasiness prevailed. The faster they wanted to reach their son, the heavier, like lead, their legs became.

Ultimately, they reached the hospital to find so many lovely people looking after their son, along with the doctors and nurses. Some had even filled the forms and paid part of the hospital charges. Only in India, such people thrive but maybe, just a handful in a Nation of 1.25 billion just second to China which has a population that can go right round the equator, equivalent to the diameter of the earth,and still not end. Why our great country, India, cannot go ahead of the Europeon countries is the pull of the dense population and it's flourishing corruption. "Sonne, whaat is the news today?"asks Paramjit,the father. The well-groomed son from a reputed school replies "Dad dear, is there any news besides killings and money trashed away in safe havens abroad. Now son, tell me something guud (good) from the paper?" "Dad, The Jungle Book with Mogli, who you like, is running. Go see it with mum and if you go for the night show I'll also come with you. This is the only entertainment for us in India."

There is hardly any country left where China is not exporting it's multi-products –you name it and it is there, while India is exporting all it's brains that it produces in the I.I.Ts and I.I.Ms. It is very happy to keep the rusty left-overs who can easily be persuaded and dissuaded to cast votes in their favour with a handful of rupees. These are the present day emperors and kings for five years and love to crush the same hand who fed them with votes. They behave no less than kings for four years and anybody trespassing their path is put to the sword but in the fifth year the hand that was ruthless is folded, going from door to door and begging for votes and the gullible (Too willing to believe) citizens fall prey to their adroit (Skilled and clever) tactics and maneuvers and the easy access to the green-green currency notes. These easily persuaded and fooled people who always danced in the rain for they had only coins in their pockets but today wouldn't dance in the rain for fear their green currency notes would get soiled.

Shawn's parents were so delighted to see and perceive their son smiling through the tucked sheets on the bed. He had been removed from the ICU to the general ward and GOD willing would be discharged soon. Maybe, Shawn required this much, needed rest and this was GOD's wonderful way to do it – man proposes God disposes. All the new found friends had a glimmer of hope – every dark cloud has a silver lining. I always wonder what about the golden lining or the red, green, pink and blue. Did God run out of these colours or couldn't trace them in the dark. Ha, ha.

Shawn introduced all his new found friends. "This is Aftab and this is Trilok Ladla with a glitter in his eye." His parents met all of them very warmly and with a profusion of never-ending thanks.

Once again life was back to normal. The dahlias in the garden smiled back as Aftab bent down to smell it, only the honey bee that was collecting it's nectar didn't like other people protruding their noses in their affairs and would have stung it had Aftab not pulled it away from harm or else another Pinocchio would have roamed the streets of the city. These honey bees are fully aware that the people are the poachers of their honey, besides the bear who just romps into their hives for the succulent honey that he loves regardless of the numerous stings that may want to puncture his thick skin protected by a thicker fur of impenetrable hair. Trilok just smiled watching the fun between the bee and his friend, Aftab. "What a pity it missed your nose otherwise we would have had mount Everest, the highest peak in the world right here in India, instead of going to Nepal." "Okay, okay you enjoyed getting me stung, now tell me the joke you were reading on your mobile," countered his friend, Aftab. Both friends were thick as thieves and from the face of it, Shawn would join them soon to make it the proverbial triangle." Okay, okay this is my very own and not pinched from the mobile. There was a huge wedding party going on and the speaker on the mike was relentlessly, like an orator, giving out yarn after yarn much to the delight of the gathering. When the Emcee came down for dinner with the rest, he met his endless friends. One of his friends pulled him up and said" You are a real robber?" "Robber, did you say?" on the point of getting really angry.

"Yes, whenever you are on the stage you steal the show." (Smiles)

9

College Days Are Here Again.

"Hey Aftab, what day is it that we are going to college to gain a little knowledge?" as both friends zig-zagged through the market place on their phat-phati. (motor-cycle) Today is a Thursday and pay heed to the road" very much unlike the youngsters of today who are rash and care two hoots for the consequences.

They were in a buoyant mood and radiating with enthusiasm. Every boy and girl's dream of being in college was fulfilled today. Trilok Ladla shouted 'hooray' along with Aftab at the top of their voices which was echoed and reverberated by another 200 boys and girls, who were busy introducing themselves to each other. I'm Gaurav from the sands of Rajasthan and I have the gaurav (pride) to be an S.S.P's son (Senior Superintendent of Police) boasted the new-comer to all and sundry. Another immediately cut him short by announcing, "I'm Anil Sabharwal and my dad happens to be the D.M.(District Magistrate). One girl, Jaya amongst them glorified her father by drowning their pride in her meek and humble way that all must be knowing the present Defence Minister, Mr Murthy and that he was her father. Maybe, these and some others could be the big-wigs of the college whose children were here. The oft repeated quote came whistling silently through the crowd of commoners but pierced the heart of many- 'Pride goeth on horse-back grand and gay but returneth on foot and begs it's way '.

This was an umbrella that the not-so-rich take recourse to. All fell to talking and shouting once again. The richee bug had been swallowed and you could see most of the ordinary students isolating themselves from these 'swollen heads' who were just a few and the ordinary out-numbered them, not just in numbers but in the grey matter too.

The chimes of the school bell that these talented youth, who would one day shoulder the responsibility of Nation building, were so used to all their lives seemed missing like the horns of a donkey. Maybe, this was one difference between a school and a college, the other very obvious was nobody forced you to go for classes unlike the school where your parents goaded you into going. "Son when you come back from school we will go for 'Twenty thousand leagues under the sea'. Your dad has already booked the tickets" and this was an incentive totally missing in college life where they treated you at par with the grown-ups.

Except for a handful of boys and girls who were day-scholars (only in Physics and Chemistry courses), rest were all boarders who were selected for different subjects after undergoing a very competitive examination.

"What place do you come from?" inquired the warden in a very fatherly tone. "I come from Baroda, sir" "And what about you?" "I come from Patna, the capital of Bihar, sir" "And how is the place and the people?" "The place is quite developed, maybe because it is the capital but other places in Bihar are in a bad shape and so are the people but slowly and surely the economy is picking up. Sir, are you aware that the highest number of I.A.S. officers are from Bihar as are the labourers who are spread in different States of India for want of work in Bihar. "Yes, yes that is very true", confirmed the warden who was a professor in the Mechanical engineering department. " I'm sure you come from Bhutan?" "Sir, you look very confident about my country. I'm sure it's my looks that give you that feedback and yet in Bhutan I'm taken more as an Indian for my looks." "Oh, is that the reason your country sent you here for studies." "No sir, I'm the best in my country and that is why I'm here." "Gurrinder Singh, how are you? I'm sure you come from Amritsar in Punjab." "Sir, how do you know my name but I do not come from Punjab but from Delhi itself." "My dear boy, you carry that exercise book against your chest with your name printed heavily on it and you expect us not to read it" and with that caught his hand as would a loving and doting father. Not for nothing was he called the best warden in the full campus.

His wife, who was a foreigner and not attached to the college on any account except for her husband, was even more loving and would make her presence felt especially when new-comers joined the college. Even she had a son studying somewhere but would treat these new boys with a lot of love and care and even serve them delicacies that they had not seen the like of before.

"Select your partners (as though it was a marriage bureau) for two boys can be in one room," which all the freshers (1st year) resented, detested but the warden would settle this cudgel only the next day. The very first impression of such an institute was everything was done very amicably – not for nothing it had such a high pedestal and reputation in society. Those who were in this college had their collars up with pride and those who all could not make it were jealous and envious of those inside.

All the boys scuttled to their respective rooms to settle their belongings which invariably had a razor and a mirror for shaving inside a small suitcase that carried their world. What was one suitcase telling the other? I come from a very high society, only the very rich have me in their possession but the other replied the secrets that I carry inside me you will never come to know unless your master and mine become friends as thick as thieves.

There was a knock and voices of two-three boys in one accord, "Are you coming for dinner?" "If you wait for two minutes, we'll be with you, "came the reply. "Sorry, we can give you just 120 seconds." "Okay mathematician, we're on our way" came a voice from inside as the door was opened with a jerk to let them in.

"What place do you come from and what about you?"

I'm from Mumbai, the place that was earlier called Bombay. I just wonder if these politicians have no other work except sit and change names of places. Madras becomes Chennai, Bangalore takes the name Bengaluru. I do not know the abc of acting and yet I come from the land of actors where most of the Hindi movies are made. Without the movies life would be very boring in India. Indians hardly have any other form of entertainment and the prices of the tickets are simply spiraling. How can a common man afford 4-5 tickets taking his family for it? Isn't it an irony that places touching the sea, like the Arabian sea here, do not have enough drinking water. Why don't some of us pool our resources of different engineering skills to solve this problem? "You can do research on this and get your Ph.D. helping millions of people get cheap drinking water" chimed the boy who said he was from Hyderabad." I'm also from Secunderabad, the twin cities" and he came forward shaking hands with him." Just check if you two are not the lost twins like in the Kumbh mela (Fair)in Varanasi? For your information the Ardh Kumbh mela is in Haridwar." " Pheli Baar suna hai" all screamed in a jubilant mood. On the way to the Dining Hall, they were joined by many other freshers as though they were falling apart – pj did you call it, still enjoy the poor joke and increase your blood by an ounce.

10

My Ears Are Hanging-College Days Again

The Dining Hall turned out to be bigger than our expectations. "I feel it can accommodate 150 students at one time." "No I feel 200 can easily fit in "commented the second boy. The third brought his mensuration fundamentals to calculate the exact number of seats. The fourth walked the length and breadth of the hall to count the seating arrangement and the most enterprising of all, a practical sardar with a lovely turban tilted slightly for style, walked upto the manager and asked him for the number of seats in the dining hall. The most innovative and hunger driven boy was the one who collected a partitioned plate from the main counter and the waiter from the cemented serving table was ready with his huge spoon to put chicken and gravy into it after ascertaining what part of the chicken the boy preferred and giving the rarest of rare smiles to all the boys, welcoming them for the years they would be in their custody. Such a lovely atmosphere prevailed that all were simply floored. In return the boys were equally courteous to all the staff. Just imagine a day earlier the chicken was jumping in the poultry farm, pecking at seeds like bajra, wheat etc and letting it go down his throat to gain in weight. The chicken gulps the seeds and the boys gulp the chicken. I sit and sometimes think if this was the only reason God created chicken and it's life-cycle. I always try to remember somewhere that I read which even today is etched out in my brain and I would like to share it with my friends and it goes like this – 'As the deer wakes up in the Jim Corbett's Park in India, it makes sure that it has to run faster than the tiger or it will end up becoming the breakfast for the tiger.

Same way, a tiger knows if it doesn't use it's stealth and speed to hunt a deer, it will die of starvation.

We, my young boys and girls, grand papa and grand – mama with white hair with worldly knowledge of right and wrong and love oozing for your grandchildren and the other children at large, are humans and capable of thinking and earning for ourselves without hurting anyone then why this strife with each other. Can't we just sit and relax without having to raise our voices or our hands to hurt someone. Hasn't History taught us enough? Don't run too much after the geography of another country – be satisfied with the land that you have. See the case of the Japanese, till America bombarded Nagasaki and Hiroshima with the Atom Bomb, they wouldn't be quiet. Hitler of Germany had the same fate in St. Helena.

I sit and sometimes reminisce if this was the only reason why GOD created the chicken and this would be it's life-cycle for which it was created. Then why has God created us –the greedy humans? Are we also the feed or grain of someone that we are in the dark about?

"Chini- Hindi Bhai- Bhai" (Chinese and Indians are brothers) was reverberated throughout the length and breadth of our country and on the other side Chinese troops were accumulating on our borders to conquer us. It was the alert eyes of the American and Russian technology that saved us in the 1962 war. Our Prime minister, Pandit Jawaharlal Nehru was in the dark, as were the Cabinet ministers.

"Yippee, chicken and puris- what a wonderful combination" and the boys sat down to nibble and some to gobble according to their appetites. Sikdar was on the rampage while others ate like normal boys.

Sikdar – "Arre bhai, bring some puris and some chicken gravy ". " Arre yaar have some fried rice, peas and paneer curry, dal and potato and brinjal vegetables also?" "Yes yaar, (friend) I'm having that also but I simply love puris." It was a wonderful technique to solicit other peoples' interest in you and be the centre of attraction. But what if the stomach bloated and there was no mummy to give you Pudin-Hara or Digesto? (medicines). Sikdar, may have been 5' 10" but his stomach touched his back, then where did he put all the food? "Sikdar, the cooks must be tired making the puris. How many did you eat anyway?" "Yaar, I don't count while eating. But why?"

Shashi immediately jumped up. He just couldn't stop himself. "I sat opposite him and counted 26 puris going down his gullet. I sat admiring his appetite that I forgot to eat my own. I even nudged Tumbe here but he was more interested in his own food," roared Shashi.

Sikdar took no offence. He just said "Even my sister says that I got a giant in my stomach. "Everyone laughed and fell to eating the dessert, comprising of two rasgullas each, that had just arrived.

Most of the boys acknowledge that the food was good and very few "It was better than what my mom cooks at home. Only a few show-offs muttered "how they will eat this rubbish for so long". The show-offs couldn't stay there longer in pretence and nearly banged into some seniors who laughed and scoffed at the same time "Arre bhai zara dekh ke chalo, aage hi nahi, peecha bhi, (Man o man, look and walk, not just in front but at the back too) Don't worry, we are your doctors and we have a long list of treatments for all your disorders. Don't we, my friends? By the way, we'll have the introduction tonight. In the meantime, remember I'm Sukhbir Singh, he is Ahluwalia, he is Faizan Khan and he is Dhanok from th---"and they were off as though it was the last call for their flight to take off.

11

Did You Hear The Word – Ragging

"Huh! What do they think of themselves" in a quivering voice that was half choked and belied of it's strength if he could stand to his uttered statement. The freshers still sitting at the dining table, nudged each other and whispered confidentially " Tonight they are getting non-vegetarian dinner from the Taj". (a 5star Hotel) It was not a sneer but a crooked smile that escaped each other's face – as they all jumped up from their chairs to go. The chairs were not one to sneer but creaked in agony, not from the relief of getting light, for being witness to the torture year after year, month after month, day after day for almost 75-80 days of sadistic, relentless pleasure of the seniors

One place where I found ragging non-existent is Maity College. They have put placards and stuck notices at every prominent place that they don't take a very lenient view of ragging and boys and girls would be expelled, if caught. They have given exemplary punishment to show what they mean. I take my hat off to the management. Many a prestigious college banning ragging are really far from what they claim. It is only a top show for fooling the public and certainly the government has a big hand in it or how can things go unnoticed. Time and again, practically every year suicides have taken place but the government does show lip-service sympathy but no action has ever been taken. Yes, if one of the Minister's son or daughter was embroiled in such a case prompt action would follow, till then suffer it out. Some boys and girls believe, when they were ragged why to break the tradition. Others just turn a deaf ear and turn themselves the other way if any entreaties come their way for help. The colleges should be penalized and the management held responsible. Everyone concerned should be awarded their punishment irrespective of their position and watch the colour of their cheeks drain out.

There was a knock-on room number 129, B block at 10.15 pm and it grew louder by the second.

Sukhbir Singh (senior)- "How long do you take to open the door?"

Raghubir Singh (fresher)- "I was just slipping into my shirt."

Faizan (senior) – "What?"

Raghubir Singh (fresher) – "I was slipping into my shirt". He never understood what they meant.

Ahluwalia (senior) – " I was slipping into my shirt, S.I.R., now you understand."

Raghubir Singh (fresher)- Little panicky- "I was slipping into my shirt, Sir."

Dhanok (senior) – "Now you know how to address a senior."

Raghubir Singh (fresher) – "Yes Siir."

Sukhbir Singh(senior) –"Why were you slipping into your shirt? You sleep in the buff? "

Raghubir Singh (fresher)- "I was not sleeping, I was reading Sir."

Faizan(senior) – "You were slipping into your shirt; so you are a snake shedding your skin?" (kechli)

Dhanok (senior)- "What did you say your name was?"

Raghubir Singh (fresher) – "You did not ask me and I did not tell you sir."

Faizan (senior) – "Ha, ha your highness, we have to ask your name?"

Raghubir Singh (fresher) – "Sorry sir".

Dhanok (senior)- "SO your name is sorry sir."

Raghubir Singh (fresher)- "Sir, my name is Raghubir Singh. "

Ahluwalia (senior)- "So, you were singing when you were born?"

Raghubir Singh(fresher)- "No sir, Singh means lion."

Sukhbir Singh (senior)- "So, your father is a lion and maybe your mother is a tigress. Then you should be called Raghubir Liger or is it the reverse Raghubir Tigon."

Dhanok (senior) – Pointing to senior Faizan, he asked "Fresher, what is his name?"

Raghubir Singh (fresher) – "Sir, you did not tell."

Dhanok (senior) – "Go, swim to the end of the corridor and ask the fresher there for my name."

Raghubir Singh (fresher)- "There is no water in the corridor for me to swim, sir?"

Dhanok (Senior) -"Poor fellow wants a swimming pool to swim through. Get him one, yaar."

Sukhbir Singh – He took a glass of water and sprinkled it on the corridor. "Now, get on to your chest and start swimming."

Poor, Raghubir Singh, had no alternative but to get down on his fours on the ground and start swimming. He flailed his arms and tried all the techniques in the world with his legs but how far could he go.

Two freshers passed by, saw Rughubir's antics at swimming and giggled. That was enough for them to get embroiled with the seniors who caught them like fish on the hook.

Ahluwalia (senior)- "Come, come my babies teach this fresher to swim, otherwise he'll get drowned."

Faizan (senior)- "What's your name?"

Fresher (1st year)- "Sir, he is Ganguly from Assam and I'm Gaffoor, Abdul Gaffoor, from Kolkatta."

Faizan (senior) – "So, you are James Bond?"

Fresher- "No sir".

Sukhbir Singh (senior)- "But your style is same like James Bond. Doesn't he say, I'm Bond, James Bond. "

Freshers- "Sorry sir."

Ahluwalia (senior)- "Okay, James Bond sir tell me you come from Kolkatta. How did the name kolkatta come to it's existence?

"Fresher (Abdul Gaffoor)- "Sorry sir, I don't know."

2nd Fresher (Ganguly)- " Sir, I'm not sure of it's authenticity but my father who hails from Kolkatta but settled in Assam, tells this story. When the British came to Calcutta and formed the East India Company, two Britons not knowing Hindi asked two workers in their own English twang, pointing to a stack of hay, "What is the naim (name) of the plais?" (place) The illiterate workers thinking when was the hay cut, replied "KAL- Katta" (yesterday). The English were impressed with the name 'Calcutta' which is today named Kolkatta.

Sukhbir Singh (Senior) - "Wonderful indeed, but it must have been very hard for your dad to travel all the way from Kolkatta to Assam in hail-stones?"

Gangully (fresher) - "No sir, I never said hail-stones but hail which means come from."

Faizan (Senior) - "Hey, hey, so you think you are very smart and can teach us?"

Gangully (Fresher) - "Sorry sir, I did not mea- "

Dhanok (Senior)- " Shut up. You all will write our four names 500 times and show us tomorrow. Good night, no, no Good-morning "The time was 2.30 a.m. and 8 a.m. were classes.

12

HI AND BYE

Very seldom the Hi and a Bye come together. More often there is a big gap between the two and if he/she are stick-fasts and if you don't like the look of them, you just wait when the Hi will turn to Bye.

How could the poor fresher avoid the seniors who pervaded all the Halls of Residences like locusts. The seniors called it introduction and getting to know the new entrants. What the seniors never knew or feigned that the juniors were not enjoying one bit of their company. Was it like the daughter –in-law who has turned into a mother-in-law and now wants to take all the revenge she suffered as a daughter-in-law.

Ragging goes on unabated due to the apathy of the government and the management of the colleges. Every year so many suicides take place but no one near and dear for these officials to stop the forty winks they continuously take.

Senior (Rao) to a junior "Hey, where are you going?"

Junior –"To my friend's room" and under his breath "I wish I could punch his nose. "

Senior (Rao) –"Go call your friends to this room."

Fresher- "Yes sir" and an inaudible abuse, the likes of which would have made the senior red in the face.

Senior (Rao)- "Did your lips move to say something?"

Junior- "Yes sir, how sweet you are to call us to your room and waste your precious time on freshers" and again on the quiet his hands tightened into a fist to shower his fury on his rib-cage.

Five innocent juniors huddled in the room with three seniors out to have fun in such a depraved manner.

Senior (Rao) – "What's your name and where do you come from?"

Fresher (Murlidhar)- "Sir, in the dining hall I told you I'm Murlidhar from Malegoan "and conspicuously missing on his tongue and on his face were abuses in capital letters from A to Z that my hands shiver to write leave alone pronouncing it for your ear-drums, so that you could join in with your electric guitar.

Senior (Lamba)- "This boy got venom of the cobra on his tongue. I have to send him to Mussoorie to cool it and on the fresher' s mind was playing "If only I could send him to hell so that he gets blisters on his tongue that no doctors could heal. Senior –"Go climb up the cemented shelf (pointing to one corner) and perch yourself up crowing like a cock."

Fresher (Murlidhar) – "Yes sir" as he climbed up gnashing his teeth. Poor boy, at such an early age, nearly lost his sparkling white teeth, not from pyrrhoea, but from gnashing his teeth.

Senior(Babu) –"What name your father, mother gave you dear?" pointing an accusing finger at Amit as though he was not born out of wed-lock.

Fresher (Amit Gowda)- "My mother calls me Amit and my father gave me Gowda – Amit Gowda from Bikaner, Sir.

Senior(Lamba) –"Indeed humorous and for that you'll bring us cold water in that jug?"

Fresher (Amit Gowda)- "Sir, from where do we get cold water?"

Seniors- "Become detective Sherlock Holmes and find out".

Fresher (Amit Gowda)- "Sure sir," and lisped softly "Wait till I put dirt in the water for you all to die of jaundice. The doctor will play Sherlock Holmes and get nowhere while you turn yellow and yellower". Fortunately, no one heard except his own bat ears. Off he trotted with the jug as though he was a horse on his majesty errands, only he did not snort and neigh as horses do.

Senior(Lamba)- "Sarkar, what's your name?"

Fresher (Sarkar) –"Sir, how do you know my name?"

Senior (Lamba) –"Your name, What's your name?"

Fresher(Sarkar)- "Sarkar sir."

Senior (Rao)- "Sarkar sir, what? Complete your sentence and don't talk in puzzles. "

Fresher (Sarkar)- "Sir, my name is Abhijeet Sarkar and I'm from Jamshedpur. My father works as the chief engineer with the Tatas. I have one brother and one sister studying in VI and VIII in the convent school there. My mother is a teacher and she has 69 children in her class. The school is affiliated to--------"

Senior (Rao)-"Shut up, shaaut up. Another word and---"

Fresher (Sarkar) –"Sorry sir" and under his breath "Mad people, don't talk they lambaste you with words. Talk, they shut your mouth with maggots(worms) eek!"

Senior (Basu) –"Sarkar, you got two options – either polish our shoes and give it that army shine or go out on the balcony and abuse each and every passerby with the choicest ones you fancy, Don't leave any son of a gun. You invent new ones that haven't seen the light of day. You may get a Ph.D. for that. Now get going."

Senior (Rao) – "Lazy louts, you two, come forward. Where do you both come from?"

Freshers – (Both Aftab and Shawn in one accord) – "We are both from St.Francis School and are from Lajpat Nagar in Delhi."

Senior (Lamba)- "So, you have seen all the lanes and bylanes of Delhi and did you come to this college before or saw it from outside, since you are from here only. Have you ever flown from the 2nd floor to the ground below." Both seniors, Babu and Rao, join in with a sinister look. Both were enjoying their suffering sadistically. "Now move on."

Without warning, both Shawn and Aftab opened the back door and flung themselves down, plummeting in the air to the ground below.

The three seniors were stumped. Their sadistic joy had turned to despair and they were drenched from head to toe not in perspiration, but in horse's sweat. What a fiasco! The colour of their blood had turned white, not a vestige of red was in sight, so it seemed from the look of their faces.

The freshers (Shawn and Aftab) must be lying sprawled in a pool of blood, wriggling in suffocation for the last breath of life. They could not face the music anymore. The Director would just throw them out of the college, possibly the fresher's parents would gouge their eyes out. The police would be ready with handcuffs and the Judge would be announcing his verdict of life-imprisonment or death by hanging to the three seniors for the murder of two freshers for ragging them to their end.

The three seniors were on pins and needles (the Mussoorie fresher from the top of the shelf wished he had real pins and needles to poke their bursting bums to turn them into real pin-cushions. The fresher cobbler or rather shoe-shine looked up from his shoes in disgust to polish the seniors' faces with black and parade them through the college. The magma inside the fresher's volcano seethed with anger but as the lava poured out in the open, the anger was a damp-squib too frightened to resonate or show it's presence.

There was nothing for the three to accede to, except death. Slowly all three seniors held hands in death and crawled towards the back door to follow the same instructions they had given their juniors, maybe in fun, but which had turned into a tragedy with repercussions that would bring shame to them, to their families and to their college. The three stood holding each other's hand tighter which were slippery as an eel with moisture of shame and wickedness. They painfully walked to the edge of the back balcony where the two juniors had taken refuge in death on their command, closed their eyes till they saw the GOD of death looming over their head, inviting them to proceed and satisfied that HE had taken a toll of five humans. One, the seniors grip on each other's hand became tighter. Two, it nearly froze each other's hand and before they could say three, the mask that the executioner puts before the rope gets taut, to squeeze out the life, found it's way on their faces.

Everything looked dark and empty and over and then there was a sudden, huge cry as the front door was pushed open "SIR" with Shawn and Aftab (freshers) stumbling over each other on the front doorway.

It took time for the seniors, Babu, Lamba and Rao to soak in the situation. The blood flowed again that had congealed and it was the prettiest red colour in the world that brought back life. The grip of the hands really slipped like olive oil had been poured onto their palms and they found themselves sobbing on the broad shoulders of Shawn and Aftab who had a quizzical look of consternation. (surprise)

What a relief! Not what you get after visiting the washroom.

13

Ragging Is Ragging

The story is almost identical with any college you take in India. ST. ZEPHEN takes the freshers out for a walk in the woods. It is for any roving eye a wonderful experience, almost like taking a family out to Jim Corbett's park. People spend thousands of rupees to have a glimpse of the tiger in the wild but with all safety precautions. They have guides and guards well equipped to save anyone in times of any attack by the wild animals. Zephenians take the freshers out in the dead of night, somewhere around 2-3 A.M., to frighten their guts out. You call it a lovely introduction of the juniors and the seniors. Why in the wild? Why not in the safety of the college's auditorium in the presence of the professors? Can't do it, my boy, you'll be expelled out of the college, the next day with the treatment you extol to the innocent freshers, just out of school. If the left road is wrong, take to the right.

I feel pity for the Creater who must have really worked hard in casting moulds for the different faces and structures and yet all in the category of the human species, in the heat of the foundry.

Take the Romans and the Spartans with their bridge of the noses high, high enough to come in the way of kissing, so we feel but in reality, it only comes in the affairs of other people, especially the neighbours and normally ladies hold this jurisdiction and men are not allowed on this turf. Most men love to sniff around while ladies go poking their noses everywhere. Both these traits are very dangerous and can lead to a big flare-up if they don't go unnoticed.

How easy it is to tell whether this spy is from Africa, Japan, Europe or India by just analyzing the features of the person. Short and rugged men are found a lot on mountain terrain where life is tough and a lot of walking is to be done.

I was talking of ragging and I will now stick to it.

The situation in the Girl's hostel was no better than the boys' hostel. When this fragile species, the girls, cannot dig their finger nails into the boys' flesh for which they are born and carry their expertise from generation to generation, never to falter, they claw the next best object, the freshers.

Senior (Shruti to freshers)-"See how chikni (smooth) you look with half the bottle of coconut oil on your head".

Fresher (Gayatri) – "Ma'am you don't put oil and yet your ha-- "

Senior (Shruti) – "Shut up, you don't ask questions, only answer what is asked? Rupenzel, Rupenzel let down your hair, we are here to make your hair long like Rupenzel "

Fresher (Gayatri) – "Who is Rupenzel? I'm Gayatri."

Senior (Zeba) – "Stupid woman, doesn't even know that and why are your slippers in their right position? Don't you know the rules of the hostel for freshers, right slipper on the left foot and left slipper on the right. "

Senior (Pavani) "And why is your salwar-kameez not inside out? Why you don't want to show and wash your linen in public?"

Fresher (Gayatri)- "Sorry ma'am" and bursting inside "wish I could wash her in public without her linen" and somebody inside her urged (Maybe her conscience) "You mean, wash her absolutely raw in public?" "Yes bhai yes, what else? and shut up, you could be heard."

Not in the beauty parlour but in the parlour of the girl's hostel where parents are welcome.

Senior (Sweetie) – "Welcome aunty, how sweet your daughter is, as though butter wouldn't melt in her mouth. Can I get you some waa-ter, aunty?"

Aunty – "No beta, thank you. How sweet of you, only look after my daughter. I heard ragging is very severe here and I'm so scared to leave her."

Senior (Sweetie) –"No auntie- with pouting lips and a very innocent face that anyone gullible would fall prey to it – seniors are so friendly here, helping the new-comers with their old notes. Media has given the shape of a monster to ragging, a mountain out of a mole hill. Aunty, why don't you stay here for a day and see for yourself? And baby, what is your name?" (pointing to the daughter)

Fresher (Pankhuri) – "My name, what my mamma and daddy call me with is, Phankuri and I go flying in their arms when they call me and what solace you get in their arms, don't you?"

Senior (Sweetie)- "Oh my, what a pet. Ooh,my,my".

Auntie- "So I think, I can go in peace. "

Senior (Sweetie) –"Rest assured, please go in peace aunty and we are there to look after her," and inside, on the computer of her brain – "We'll rip her apart in pieces, just you wait and see, dear aunty, dear auntie."

Poor gullible, aunty that she was, took every word and the senior's sweetness as Gospel truth, hugged her daughter and even the senior, without realizing the venom she carried for her darling daughter. The sixth sense of Mrs. Jhunjhunwala, the mother of Pankhuri, had gone out grazing – so you think Pankhuri's mother was a cow? How else would she go grazing? Usually, what the ladies say, do or mean are all different, but here were two ladies, one to match the other with their management skills – one of the old school and one of the new. It was clear here, the younger generation was superior. Understanding a man is child's play compared to understanding the lady – she is riddled with complexes, beyond the comprehension of man. A measure of it can be seen in any husband trying to understand his wife and in the end just giving up but here the fight was between two cats, not the ones that purr, but the ones who make their husbands dance to their peculiar tunes all their lives. A very devoted and lallu husband was heard saying "I never heard any tune escaping my wife's lips and I have never danced all my life, having two left legs. Then what tune are they talking about?"

Senior(Sweetie) –"Come my pet, you are now in a lion's den. "

Fresher (Pankhuri) – "This is not a zoo."

Senior(Sweetie) – "Just you wait, how we peel your dermis and leave the raw epidermis looking shaken and shamefully unclothed."

Fresher (Pankhuri)- "But you told my mother you'll save me from all this?"

Senior (Sweetie)- " Your mother would have taken you back, so I coaxed her out of it. Hullo Meher, (senior) as she came in, Here's another toy for us tonight, to play with."

Fresher(Pankhuri) realized she was in deep hot water and there was no escape. She, like the ostrich, could not bury her head in the sand to escape. The thought of putting resistance did not register on her mind. She had grey matter which had brought her to this eminent college. What eminence was this that seniors and juniors had to have it out with juniors being the silent spectators and sufferers and seniors only enjoying the show. She took heart from the fact that she was not the only stupid girl not retaliating, but other freshers were along with her.

Senior (Sweetie)- " For a beginning, go to all the rooms on this floor and get as many names of the occupants?"

It is a Sunday morning. All the freshers are lined up in their outfits of inside out salwar kameez. The slippers straining to get onto the right foot but who dared restrain the order of the seniors. Inside every fresher was boiling but none dare bring it on their lips. Lips were sealed as though never to open. Were all the seniors Hitlers? Nazi rule had not died down altogether – it was reborn in a country like India, which to some outsiders, apparently, would look a very rich nation for Indians drinking tea on a train would invariably throw the cups they were drinking tea in, out of the windows. What these foreigners never knew was that these cups (Kullads) were made of mud.

A begging bowl adorned each fresher. "Not a single abuse will escape your lips, you B------, you --------, you----, screeched the general secretary of the hostel, with a mouth that even smelt of the dirtiest abuses.

They all walked in a single file to the market place with seniors throwing abuses as though they were petals of flowers.

"See these girls, how funny they look?" screamed a mother to her grown –up daughter, looking straight into them with piercing eyes.

"Mum they are girls from the nearby college and they are being ragged. See the oil pouring from the braids, how funny the inside –out salwar kameez looks and see the chappals on opposite feet. How ridiculous the begging bowls? " The onlookers ogled their eyes out, as the market place seethed with repeated laughter at the sight.

Two young girls couldn't contain their laughter seeing a fresher being forced to beg for a half-eaten ice-cream.

The crowd of buyers in the market place burst into a frenzy of loud laughter, a quiet smile by a docile and shy lady, who most likely was remembering her own time in college but the one I'm narrating now is out of the blues.

"Sir", as a fresher fell on her knees infront of a handsome boy," this rose is for the years of love I have for you and today I offer my hand in marriage " as she placed her hands in his. The boy looked a senior from another college who had a bath of humour and now wanted to tickle the funny bone of everyone in the market – " I would love to clasp and hold such lovely hands for life but who will hold the other part of the body for life?" The crowd went berserk with deafening noise as some freshers, the sensitive type, quietly rubbed the tears of humiliation from their eyes; some cried openly while others sobbed on the quiet with their conscience openly protesting inaudibly- "I'll rob this senior of her husband, then she'll understand the real pain of humiliation." The inner voice seemed to laugh but her face was wry, not with a crooked smile, but with fear.

One man's pain is another man's gain, so we found today.

"Mamma, I'm feeling hungry. You are again and again telling me daddy will come with money and then you will give me milk to drink but he is still not coming. Baby has already slept off without food. Are we going to get any food today?" This is a cry coming from a lot of remote corners of the world but do we have ears to hear? And even if we can see, we hate to perceive it – some pretend not to hear, others just turn their faces away- "Oh, they are beggars and they will always cry, such is their fate." Have we all become so insensitive, has our skin become so thick that there are no feelings for them. What if our children cried for food and we had nothing to give. The world is so big that a quarter of it's people are crying incessantly (constantly) with hunger and praying to a deaf and dumb God who preys on them, especially the very poor without mercy. I don't want government figures to show where we are headed. Just walk into any lane or by-lane and see the wailing of the poor. Sorry, for such an imprudent thinking. The poor are only born to suffer and this world is no place for them.

In another part of the world, people are dancing to some weird music, weird for us and really palatable for them. There is a wedding on with bliss for two days and blisters for the rest of their lives. Inspite of this short lived happiness we love to fight, cantankerous that we are by nature, greed that can never fill our coffers and then there is a call from 'Above' to leave everything and go.

"Come dance in the rain, asks a poor man to the rich. "No, no you got coins which won't get wet, so you can dance but I got green-green notes which will get soiled and so I'm scared."

Amidst all this dwindling happiness and everlasting misery, life goes on unabated with thousand questions asked and none answered and why should anyone stand in a queue to even remotely answer. All this time wave after wave comes kissing the sea shore as would a child his mother.

Ragging raged for two and a half months and stopped as suddenly because of the approaching examinations. Ragging is something dreadful for those who go through this hell-fire but wonderful for those who watch in person or read it in books like the one you are holding right now.

"Hey, did you hear a fresher in Einstein's hostel committed suicide due to ragging last night? What will happen now?" " Nothing much yaar, he is not a minister's son or even our principal's son for them to be worried. Such apathy is in abundance in every college all over India and the government just does lip-service that it is doing everything in it's power to stop ragging. "Don't eat pan-masala, it will give you cancer. Don't smoke cigarettes, it will cause lung cancer. Just stop their production but they levy heavy taxes on it and to get the splurge why should they stop such lucrative business and especially when the same people are helping them win the battle of the ballots by pumping in millions of rupees to give to the poor to get their votes –insignificant in front of the crispy notes for the poor and a mine of treasure and very significant for the elected minister."

"Arre yaar, who doesn't know all this? I was just holding my breath for your Majesty to finish your speech. Aditya, I feel you can become a lovely politician. I feel you have selected the wrong vocation. Join politics and one vote is for sure from my side." "I do think I should do something for my country and it's people but my dad tells me honesty and politics do not go hand in hand and in the long run I will suffer. I did want to root out corruption but now I have reconciled to my present work, like millions of boys and girls who had a spurt of uneasiness and then it died.

After the examination, there was a break of ten days and the hostels bore a deserted look. So, I have come to the conclusion that it is humans, the boys and girls, the men who work to feed the different mouths, the professors who impart knowledge and other associated people who are the real flowers and bouquets who enliven and decorate any place. The Valley of Flowers, close to Simla and Dharamshala would be bereft of any beauty till a human eye winks at it's magnificence. A peacock dancing in the rain with it's tail spread out in the wild goes unnoticed till the retina of the eye of a human clicks a picture on its magnificent camera for life.

14

SOMETHING TO TALK ABOUT FOR LIFE

Pankhuri Jhunjhunwala was going by Assam Mail with two of her friends, Azra and Sharmelee, to Darjeeling where her parents would arrive next day.

Pankhuri –"Lazy bone, you still sleeping. Don't you know we have to reach the station on time. Get up or I'll douse you with cold water from the water cooler."

Sharmelee – "Let me sleep, you jackass! Last night also you kept on jabbering with the gift of the gab that you carry loosely on your tongue. Doesn't it ever get tired and needs rest. Forty more winks and I'll be with you both. Azra had started counting 1, 2, 3,4-------- out of fun while Sharmelee slept like a log of wood and was back to snoring in seconds as though she had sold all her horses. (Magic indeed, a girl turning into a log of wood and I never heard of logs of wood going to sleep, did you? Did anywhere earlier they mentioned that Sharmelee was the owner of a stud-farm, then how in her sleep did she sell all the horses – intriguing? ". Poor Azra was left with the duty of winking and counting forty times before she could gather her wits and guts to coax Sharmelee out of her sleep. A cab was called from the taxi-stand.

A sleepy old driver came with an equally old taxi in a dilapidated condition with the bonnet on the engine completely missing.

Azra - "Where is the bonnet of the car and will this taxi reach the railway station today?"

Driver – "I removed the bonnet (head) so that it never gets hot even when we talk bad things about it and ma'am it has reached big,big people beyond their destinations and you are such small fries."

Pankhuri – "Okay, ok, hold your tongue."

Azra – "Poor fellow, if he holds his tongue with his hands, how will he drive?" All three burst out giggling – giggles are mainly a girl's right whereas boys have a hearty laugh. If girls are playing basket-ball, hands are used less for passing the ball. It is the giggles and shrieks that frightens the ball from one side to the other.Don't take offence my dear girls –how can you live in the water and be enemies with the crocodile and I live in the water with a girl (my dahling wife) who has the traits of both a crocodile and an alligator. (She takes it very sportingly and her 'woof' is worse than her bite".

All three flung their small, precious suit-cases in the dicky and sat in the taxi. The driver, with the small nose which sat in a slant on his funny but humourous face, put the key in the ignition and forgot to turn it for he was busy admiring the three works of the Lord in his car and enjoying every word that slipped out from their spittled tongue into the air and onto his welcoming ear-drums. If he had the sticks to play the drums, he certainly would have added the drum-beat. (okay, pj)

Sharmelee – "When will you start the taxi or you want us to break a coconut for good omen."

Taxi driver –"Ma'am, it is not starting."

Sharmelee – "Without turning the ignition key, how do you expect the taxi to start?" All three giggled, till the roof and the ceiling of the taxi caved in. "What a lovely start to a lovely journey, "all chorused in unison. All three were in their elements. Now don't ask me which elements? Sodium and potassium I'm sure, others you take a wild guess? Another, maybe, laughing gas but elements you settle yourself.

The engine of the taxi spluttered, purred and then it was dead, as though it was a human.

Pankhuri – "Hey dude, what's up?"

Taxi driver – " Maybe the engine is toooo hot. Can I get some waater?" The excited girls produced two of their own, cold drinking water bottles. The taxi driver drank two sips, keeping the bottle at arm's length as though a shop-keeper was cooling the hot milk in kullads (earthen pots) to serve to the impatient waiting cutomers. The rest of the water he poured on the engine which hissed in protest with steam gurgling out in anger for it was just exhausted. Fortunately, God never gave it a tongue or else it would have lambasted the driver.

Half-way through the journey the girl's shouted "SMOOKE" and sure enough smoke was billowing out from the crevices of the missing bonnet of the car. The taxi driver put the taxi at the side of the road and ran for water for the car to cool down. However, the girls refused to go further with him, so he stopped a passing taxi and helped them get in. Sweet of him to help people who were discarding him. This is India my boy, with people always ready to help.

The Assam Mail had tea leaves plastered all over with an Assamese offering a cup of tea, to bolster and prod you into buying Assam tea just as any company would do to advertise it's products. The three girls, our very own Pankhuri, Azra and Sharmelee along with all shades of people, totaling 72 berths in this compartment- B1- alone, ensconced themselves in comfort that this train could offer. The usual scene of any place on any platform in India was clearly visible and yet invisible because of the huge crowd that manifests itself everywhere. Just focus your eyes on the second biggest island in the world- Australia –(the first being Greenland) where only three passengers travelled on the train. Those who are looking for only comfort must go to Australia and those who want to talk to people, stay in India and pass your time talking. My dear boy, solitary confinement is the worst punishment anyone can ever get.

The Assam Mail pulled out of the platform after much chain pulling and after a wait of half an hour for a very insignificant M.L.A. (member of Legislative assembly), who had no right of putting people to inconvenience. The train was running at 120 km/hr when the black coat of a TTE (train ticket examiner) appeared.

TTE – "Tickets please"

All dived into their bags as though it was a swimming pool and retrieved the tickets only Sharmelee couldn't trace where her ticket was. Fortunately, her name was on the confirmed ticket's list but the stern TTE wanted her to pay 25% of the ticket to issue a new one. Some passengers even tried that he take Rs 100/ as bribe as is usual on the trains but he was extremely honest and wouldn't listen to all the entreaties of the girls and some sympathizers till a policeman on duty with a rifle came to their rescue. "Arre yaar TTE sahib, don't you see innocent students, don't you have children? Just think they are yours and forget the issue and anyway her name is on the list. The stern TTE softened a bit and what his face showed changed completely as though he was a chameleon. Instead of paying 25% you all will hear the joke that I crack. It is my very own joke but my children refuse to hear them. Two boys aged 12-13 years were fighting. One angry boy to the other "I'll give you a box." 2nd boy –" Okay, I'll keep my clothes in it."

"He's a jolly good fellow, He's a jolly good fellow, He's a jolly good fellow, so say all of us" the three girls sang lustily and loud till half the compartment was pulled with the magnetic effect it had on them.

They played 'Beggar my neighbour' and 'whist drive' (cards) with the passengers and the journey was such a hit.

Close to Kanpur, Sharmelee felt cold because of the Air-conditioning temperature being set too low and asked Pankhuri to pass her small suit-case. Pankhuri found Azra's suit-case and her own but there was no trace of Sharmelee's suit-case. The full compartment came to their rescue, searched under the berths, searched in the bath-rooms and in the passage, but no sign of it anywhere. They resigned to their fate and waited for the TTE to make a report and maybe, an FIR.(first information report)

Tea and biscuits were served and they sat dunking (to put biscuits into tea quickly before eating it) biscuits in the tea with funny suggestions to retrieve the stroller.

"How can a stroller get lost on a running train?" all enquired of the TTE when he came. Seeing Sharmelee "You again. First you loose your ticket and now this. You liked my 1st joke that you want to hear another one or is this serious that you really lost your suit-case? I heard walls have ears but did your stroller have feet to run out of the train? I'll have to call the railway protection force (RPF) to look after you or I'll be held responsible if something happens to you. "He called for the RPF and two personnel with loose shorts walked in reluctantly. They hit the stick here and there hoping, maybe, to frighten the suit-case to come out of it's hiding- Playing 'hide and seek' but with who? They were clueless as is the usual case for the thieves who are in race with them are atleast 100 years ahead of them. Such clever people who devised new ways to hoodwink the people and the police should be utilized in the right direction. Just see this brain. you go and fill petrol in your car and you are given a key chain free of cost. You grab it because it is free. What you do not know that it is an electronic device giving information about your address to them. Do they want to meet you to shake hands with you? My foot, they want to rob you. Be alert.

One old gentleman with grey hair showing experience, at almost the end of the compartment with 72 berths, pulled out a box and asked "Whooose?" and the owner claimed it. Taking cue from this, the RPF personnel pulled out each and every box to find the owner.

"What was the colour of your suit-case? " the RPF fellows inquired.

"It is blue." Sharmelee replied. They pulled all the blue ones but got no nod.

One huge suitcase looked weird and out of place but when the girls said "No" they pushed it back in place.

The detective, Sherlock Holmes amongst them, the wise old gentleman seeing the ungainly suitcase inquired repeatedly "Who is the owner of this huge suitcase"? but got no reply. The RPF men's suspicions were raised and they once again pulled out the huge suitcase. Very carefully they opened it fearing it could have a bomb and lo and behold the blue stroller was peeping out from inside the huge suitcase and shouting that it nearly died of suffocation.

What a clever way for this trickster to adopt, but maybe, he had already slipped away. I, once again, take my hat off to show my bald head, for this thief and his ingenious ways. Wish he had used his ingenuity for better things and the government must take cognizance of it and sure enough people would have paid 'salaams' to him instead of him cooling his heels in the prison. I, now recollect someone readily and happily agreeing to my bald head – I now want them to come forward and count the number of hair on my slippery head. Failed eh!

15

Absorb All The Happiness You Can And Give Some To Others

"Raise all the dust you can

Before you lie down

And the dust on you. " ---- written by Arnold Iwin Francis and his belief on life and happiness.

The Toy-train from New Jalpaiguri to Darjeeling really absorbs you.

Pankhuri – "What a picturesque scenery. See the flowers blooming everywhere, some even peeping through the windows,to say 'Hello and welcome to Darjeeling' as the wind sways them in."

Azra and Sharmelee in almost one voice – " We are watching every detail and enjoying it to the hilt, besides absorbing it to carry home. We must bring our parents here and I'm sure they will enjoy too much –no three much- unfortunately, we don't enjoy too much with them as we friends enjoy with each other. Don't do this, don't do that, you will get hurt – they treat us like babies. What they forget, we can create babies now.

Pankhuri – "Okay, okay enough of your nonsence, how about searching for the creater, now that we are going to Darjeeling.

Sharmelee – "What creater? Creater in Darjeeling! What are you talking about?"

Azra –"Dumb –ass, had it been an astronomical mathematics sum, you would have been the first to solve it but ordinary day –to-day life you fail miserably. We are talking of boys, handsome boys, macho boys. They are the ones, to make flat and take out their air. Don't they show-off too much?"

Sharmelee- "Okay, okay I remember seeing a movie where this super-star met his girl on the train, when he was driving to Darjeeling in his army jeep."

Pankhuri – "Stop wool-gathering, it was Rajesh Khana in-----------------"

Azra – "It is not Rajesh Kha-na but Rajesh Khanna in Aradhana."

The 'Ghoom Curve' was such a delight to watch in reality

and the best part is the road runs parallel to the railway tracks and you can wave your hand to travelers in cars and motor-cycles.

Sharmelee – "Pankhuri, see that dude waving to us."

Pankhuri – "Wave back and see him leaving his bike and climbing into our compartment?"

Azra – (scared) –"Leave him alone. What if he really gets into our compartment?"

Pankhuri – "If he does, we'll tell him you are the one who was waving."

The usual giggle of girls filled the coach.

I always wonder where this 'giggle' vanishes once these same girls get married? Is too much responsibility put on their delicate shoulders? Are the in-laws to be blamed or are her dreams too high for reality to be cowed down to shoe level. Whatever it be, the shine of a new marriage soon gets dull for both boys and girls unless there is a lot of love between the two. Inanimate objects like shoes also need polish to shine and here are two humans with roving eyes to admire the next works of God.

Small stations kept showing every 2-3 kilometers and the small engine, a beauty to look at, guzzled kiloliters of water at every step to keep itself cool from passing overtures at all and sundry.

Azra – "Hey the train is running back. Yes, indeed it is!

Pankhuri and Sharmelee looked out of the window, as did others, and saw the train was actually running down. Panic gripped the passengers for they thought the train was out of control of the driver. All hell broke loose for they thought the train would run down-hill without stopping and bang into something and which would be the end of all. Fortunately, for some elderly people who had travelled many times on this stretch and the TTE, this catastrophe was averted on time for some youngsters were already hanging on the windows and dangling. The train came to a halt but only after traversing 2-3 kilometers.

Passengers were all out on the hill-side remembering their mother and father for only in times of trouble do we, humans, remember them and the ALMIGHTY. All safe on the ground were inquiring from each other "What happened?"

"There is no coal left for the engine to run. It seems the driver sold all the coal to the wayside people, who hold Rs2 or 5 or any other denomination on a long stick and accordingly the coal is pushed down from the engine for the buyers who collect it. He bought booze to drink and now he is drunk to the brim."

The guard was seen collecting dry branches and twigs to run the engine. People joined in. It was fun collecting old tyres, breaking branches of trees, Coco cola, Pepsi bottles and paper. The acrid (unpleasant smell) smoke from burning tyres did hurt the eye but everyone was excited and happy that they had helped in running the engine. When all hands join for any work be sure it will have to be successful as it was here for the engine to pull to the next station where it was refilled with coal.

As the engine picked up speed, a fat husband and a fat wife could be seen running to catch the train.

"Oye, mota, moti ko dekho " everyone screamed.

The guard and driver were in their element and enjoyed the scene equally by increasing the speed of the train. They halted at a distance for the couple to get in. Everyone roared with laughter including the couple. That's life, my dear boys and girls. Don't grumble, just enjoy even if the joke is on you. It is not everyday that you get a chance to have a race with the train and then to make a train –load of people roar with laughter, which is the hardest thing in the world. Just try making people laugh, possibly only a frown will greet you and then you will understand what I mean.

"At the passing out parade in the Air-Force around noon, this particular officer was decorated with 'wings' to fly planes henceforth and the same day in the late evening, he was getting married to his long-time girl-friend.

Never heard of getting 'wings' in the morning, to be cut off in the evening the same day.

I laughed at this borrowed joke but tell me truly, did you? Possibly, not a frown creased your forehead, leave alone a smile and laughter is out of bounds. Laugh at your ills and save doctor's bills – heard from childhood but never adhered to. Why do you see a line of patients waiting at the doctors – some few very serious which is out of our ambit and the majority who just refuse to laugh and if there is a smile it is a constipated one.

A new family, hot from the oven, with only women-folk entered the compartment. Being all girls of different ages, they had an altercation and squabble with a young handsome boy seated opposite our giggling girls Pankhuri, Azra and Sharmelee and which boy would want to relinquish his seat having the company of such lovely girls. Maybe just enjoying the three ivory works of the LORD and their suave tongue and the new entrants did not savour in his favour.

Eldest girl- "These days boys do not have the courtesy to offer their seats to girls? Has chivalry amongst the boys flown out of the window?" (some girls who had quietly been drooling on this handsome boy's sight, gnashed their teeth and wished "Why doesn't he really throw them out of the window? Good riddance to bad rubbish). Everyone present, realized the callous(indifferent) disregard this girl had for other's feelings- everyone nodded their heads in agreement without even shaking their head. The quiet enjoyment of approval is more fun than when it is boisterous. I'm sure, my lovely readers, must have had such occasions somewhere or the other in life and treasured it to share with their near and dear ones, in the secrecy of their homes. No place in the world can be better than your home where you can scratch yourself freely without feeling ashamed.

This world is a seething cauldron of emotions- some like this cantankerous (bad tempered) and effusive (too much emotion) young lady and the other, like the boy, cool as a cucumber. Wish all the world was like him, there would never be fights. It takes two hands to clap and what a wonderful world it would be to live in.

Long after the scene was enacted and over, Pankhuri was nudging her friends, like an unusually, usual girl, that this girl looked every inch a B.T.M.(benji turned mod) in a whisper that would have been audible, had the train been running on graves? Wasn't the train running on sleepers?

Sick joke did you say? Then go see a doctor – you need his services.

Another family sitting at the far end were heard (if you strained your ears) "I think the train belongs to her father. I wonder if they have even bought their tickets? We'll wait and watch when the ticket collector comes."

He did not come but a replacement of his, did. It was a mad lady who nearly sat in the B.T.M's lap. The B.T.M. got such a scare that she jumped from her seat and landed in the same boy's lap who she was fighting with. He cuddled her tight, like a baby, in his own protective way while the mad lady sat twitching her nose and her shivering mouth kept telling tales, no one could hear but wished they could decipher and understand her tongue. I'm sure, there are people who even today, are trying to decode her speech that she never uttered and trying to bemuse their families with it. It is an art to make a mountain of a mole hill. This is life and this is the way we amuse and belittle others to get a thrill in our lives. Isn't that, what I'm doing right now? Sure, sure, that's what all authors do and I may be the biggest ass (donkey) around. Don't close your ears to my braying? Danchu, danchu! Are we happy now? Let's continue.

All the ladies, girls were petrified and the men and big boys tried to wear a bold look when inside their pants they were shivering. They wanted to keep their hands off her but all on-lookers saw the girls had ceded their territory and were happily ensconced three in one seat.

The mad woman sat mumbling and twitching her nose and the cheeks on her face rose and fell alternately, one at a time. It is so nice to watch such things on television without a trivial thought but certainly not so in real, face to face.

Suddenly she jumped onto her feet, trotted like a horse to the door of the compartment, flung it open, hung like a bat, only not in an upside down position, to the railing of the compartment till a passing electric pole hit her on the nose. She was bleeding profusely and put her tongue forward to lick it. She looked a perfect picture of a vampire with red blood trickling all over. Who could and would help a mad woman? It was a scene, just sad and yet hilarious that she made out of it.

Instead of helping, there was an exodus of passengers into the next compartment as though refugees were fleeing the country due to partition.

The toy train is a dream come true and wow! Darjeeling is a darling of all visitors and honey-mooners.

We may be effusive in our words of praise for Darjeeling but it would look like butter wouldn't melt in our mouth if we didn't speak the truth.

16

SHAWN GOES TO MUSSOORIE

Mussoorie, the queen of hills, is well known throughout India, not just because I.A.S. (Indian Administrative services) Academy is located here producing some of the finest officers who take on the onerous task of being Commissioners, D.M's (district Magistrate) etc, etc. but also because of it's cool locale, being around 6000 feet above sea level, as are the other Hill stations.

How frightening it must be to live in a place

which is just 3 meters (around 9 feet 9 inches) above sea-level. Anytime, the sea wishes to embrace the island from heel to toe it will smother the full land in it's wavy kisses. Will the inhabitants return their kisses with a tighter smooch and equally tighter squeeze. Only these words will surface, the rest will lie in a watery bosom, never to use their nostrils again. I just hope the seas and oceans don't ever show their eagerness to love, like the Black Widow spider who eats the male after their love session.

I was so much into happiness and joy then how did death stealthily take it's place. This is the hardest truth that man has to undergo. Joy and happiness of birth have to be reconciled with the coldest misery of death.

Maybe, the men and women of this world would become irrefutably wicked but death places a hand to bring in equilibrium. Whatever you have earned legally, illegally in this life, the cold hands of death will snatch it in a jiffy to leave you stranded, gasping for breath.

Help the poor when you can even with the smallest dime (money) for there won't be time for regret. I won't say more for the younger generation is far, far superior than all of us – oldies, happy to hear that sound but that's what I am. I can reverse the digits of 61 to make it sweet sixteen (16) but HIS clock runs automatically without a shake.

Shawn forced his father and mother to come with him to Mussoorie but they declined with the excuse that dad has work and mum has to prepare his food time to time. They literally forced him to take his friends and go for 4-5 days. His friends told him "the old lady and his dad want time for themselves" and they all had a good laugh. Shawn believed they wanted him to enjoy with his own age-group and yet something stirred in him.

"Your son gets on my nerves sometimes when I want to be in your arms and hold you tight" whispered his mother to Mr.Singh as she fought frantically to snuggle close to Shawn's dad. "I get so exhausted at times when he refuses to sleep that I can easily throttle him." "Don't you even dare talk such things about my lovely, heart-throb son, Shawn," in quite a serious tone and next minute the mother had clasped his dad in her arms and was smothering him with kisses like a child. This scene Shawn had noticed with his eyes almost closed when both the parents felt their son, Shawn was fast asleep, when actually he was just drowsy and had not gone to sleep. Almost similar scenes with a little more like "Had he been your own ---------------" it was not very clear for Shawn had turned his side and he was not inquisitive to know. Almost similar scenes Shawn had witnessed 3-4 times and his dad rebuking the mother.

In childhood, he was too small to even think or care but later, when he grew up a little, it would traumatize him.

He would try to ask his school friends if their mother ever used the word "throttle "if they did not sleep. He would get awkward answers from the bigger boys "pretend to sleep and watch your mum and dad ".

In all the families, when the child brought a good Report Card, he was invariably the father's son and if he brought a poor Report card he was the mother's son with a retort from the father to the mother " your son has taken after you and your disgraceful family." All these things distracts any child, as it did Shawn.

"She'll be coming down the mountains when she comes, when she comes" Shawn and his friend, Vivek, were singing with all the gusto, sitting in the bus for Mussoorie.

Shawn- "Hey, are we mad to send her down while we go up. Don't we want her to be up with us?"

Vivek – "Who are you talking of? Have you invited someone? "

Shawn- "You are a real nut, don't you understand?"

Vivek – "Ofcourse, we want her up with us."

Shawn- "Wow, now which girl are you talking about?

Have you seen the bevy of beauties sitting in the front three rows. I just hope they don't get down before Mussoorie. Have you seen the wrestler like father with the nasty look but the mother looks a dainty darling with such a sweet smile. I'll get to them through her, with my adroit negotiations."

Vivek- "Hey dude, what's up? We have just started." Shawn- "Whoever gave you the name 'Vivek' never knew that it means clever for I think you are miles away from it".

Vivek –"Be precise, how much?"

Shawn – "Approximately 1,86,000 miles - the speed of light." Both burst out laughing "But boy, aren't we enjoying?" coaxed Shawn for Vivek to agree.

The not-so rickety- rackety bus ran at the speed the driver thought fit. Anyway there was no 'governor' to fix the speed of the bus which alarmed Shawn to such an extent that he asked Vivek.

Shawn- "What governor, are you talking about, Vivek?"

Vivek –"Careful, you jackass! I'm not talking of any governor from any Union Territory but the governor fitted in the bus to control the speed."

Shawn – "So, I'm a jackass! I'll knock your head off!" and once again, both burst out laughing, as though Laughing Gas was too much in the air.

The conductor was picking all and sundry from any place, as is usual in any place in India and there were a few who had even got down from the bus. The bitter –sweet truth was their front row sweet-hearts were still there cracking jokes.

Vivek- "You heard how softly they are cracking jokes?"

Shawn –"Are their jokes walnuts? But where is the hammar they crack it with?" Both did not know whether to smile or cry, so both burst out laughing. It was a season to laugh, maybe. If you have noticed or are observant, anything out of the house on a journey is fit for laughing. "See he is sleeping with his eyes open or see his bat ears?" are enough to make you roar with laughter. It is just a very few who are fully constipated and will not laugh even if the joke is full of laughing beans, ready to split even at your sight.

The bus ran,as usual, as though it was taking part in a marathon race.

The humps on the road gave the bumps to show the dirty lingerie the bus was wearing but the Mercedes cars, the BMW cars showed the lacy petticoats that they wore underneath, just as casually ladies do, in the higher hierarchy in parties and dances.

The conductor looked humorous and jovial and would let the new entrants occupy and sit comfortably before he would approach them for the ticket money.

One person entered in a hurry and flung his luggage in the middle of the adjacent seats and drew the attention of the conductor to look after the luggage while he went out to the three-wheeler on which he had arrived. He came back in a hurry asking the conductor for five hundred rupee change, which he held in his hand. He took five, hundred-hundred rupee notes and went down showing his luggage was still there, but had still not parted with his five hundred rupee currency note. The conductor was not perturbed for the luggage was there. After around five minutes the driver started honking for the conductor to give the green signal to start the bus. The conductor peeped out to hurry up the new entrant but saw no sign of him. He got down to see but there was no trace of him. He made inquiries from people standing by but nothing that could give him a clue. He told some by-standers to hurry the stranger for he could not carry on waiting for him. He had to see other passengers also and see to their comfort. After a wait of 15 minutes he got a little worried and suspicious. He opened the gunny-bag (luggage) that was tied well and found only a stack of hay inside. The imposter had flown with his five hundred rupee currency note.

Thieves are atleast a hundred years ahead of the police. They are like the tigers who have to either out-smart the deer or run faster to catch them or perish with hunger.

What ways these imposters find to defraud people. Either it is abject poverty or illiteracy that drives these abattoirs of the law to such unheard of tactics.

A smiling, happy-go-lucky conductor was agog with his own foolishness and left half paralysed in the deafening silence that ensued for all talked in very hushed voices. The only noise that rose above all, was what the needle of the tyres sang over the 33 1/3 rpm records (rotation per minute) of the road which was still treading on old surfaces and had no time to change to C.D's, DVD's or USB's. (compact discs etc)

Vivek and Shawn were students and had little pocket money, still they added Rs 50/ each and tried to give Rs 100/ - to the conductor who profusely thanked them but declined to accept. If only all have the generosity of the two boys, not a single child will ever sleep with an empty stomach. Don't you wish that day comes in your life time, dear readers? It was also the first time the beautiful girls turned around, craned their giraffe necks and put their gazelle, almond shaped eyes on the two boys. The soft gaze floored them and the inimitable smile(the smile that cannot be copied) set the two on fire. Perhaps a fire-brigade had to be called to douse such heat that would put the Sun's solar energy to shame.

The distance of around 192 kms from Delhi to Mussoorie was not a very long ride compared to Shimla, Nainital or even Manali. We had found on one of our earlier visits to Dalhousie, as the name suggests, the place was really dull and lousy, except for maybe, honey-mooners who really don't need busy lanes but the willing, loving hands of their partners. They enjoy the cool climb to the hill and the lovely warmth they carry for each other maybe God's choicest wedding gift when they take the seven pheras (rounds) around the fire with the pandit ready with his shloks or in the church when they say 'I do'.

Poor husbands become bonded labourers from that day and run around in circles (pheras) all their lives at the slightest whims and fancies of the girl. As long as the girl stays a bride she is lovely to behold and as she turns into a wife she cuts your life without a knife. The invisible leash that she carries is unbreakable and yet he is happy bringing all the black and white money and putting in her custody and coffer. "Now, now wait I want to know how you can say all this with so much certainty? Is the leash around your neck too?" "Yes yaar, yes but don't air it out so much that it reaches her ears too – God save me, not from the fires of Hell but from the screech of my wife – the bark is worse than the bite."

The plains where the majority of the people stay are like wives and the hills where you go for a short time are like your old girl-friends or new ones in the making. I can see some wives twisting their noses in disgust. My advice to them is don't twist it so much that it takes a permanent bend. The bus was actually negotiating a bend – a curve where all types of accidents take place. Everyone was inhaling the coolness and savouring the picturesque beauty with a new vigour that hills are known for.

The majestic pine trees swayed with the wind to bow at the new arrivals with a furtive (secret) glance and a welcome that only these lofty pine and fir trees are endowed with. The Hollyhocks, as though standing on stilts, would sing an inaudible song of welcome. The daisies, shy as ever, would hide in the green carpet of grass, occasionally showing their white faces, when the green hands of the grass would tire out with exertion. The lonely red rose would be ready with it's soldiers of thorns so that no naughty boy puts out his hands from the running bus to pluck it.

The climb of 20 kilometres to Mussoorie, at a height of around 6000 feet, from Dehradun is almost the steepest. The same height to Nainital is covered from it's base, Kathgodam in 36 kilometres. Simla, Manali and Darjeeling take a long detour to arrive, but Srinagar takes the cake. "Can we also have a piece of the cake?" Asks Vivek of Shawn. "Why not, but we'll have to go there to get it," replies Shawn. Almost ten hours elapse from Jammu Tawi and suddenly you are in the Srinagar valley- I'm sure it is the abode of Gods where we human weaklings are allowed to dwell, which is paradise.

Mussoorie is Mussoorie where the best gentry arrives from all parts of the world.

Shawn and Vivek found Savvy Hotel neat and clean over-looking the Mall road.

Vivek tried a cold shower but "eek it's too cold" shifted his stance to the instant geyser.

Vivek – "Mussoorie is cold yaar."

Shawn – "It was much colder when I was a small child but after commercializing the cold has receded. Ages back my parents had to buy two buckets of hot water for Re 1, or else they could not even put their hands in the cold water to wash their faces. Such was the freezing temperature in those days which the present generation will fail to understand. Why don't we start with a small peg? How's the idea?" Their white sparkling teeth, fit for an advertisement on the telly, munched and crunched the spicy French fries and the whisky as it went in, made them frisky.

Vivek- "Hey, hey, the girls from the bus. "

The girls were sitting at the corner table with glasses in their hands. The colour did not show any cold drink but it was something of a pale golden colour. They gulped it down and sizzled their way out winking at some boys.

Shawn – "Come on, let's have fun with them. See what I do? Their muscle-man is not there."

So, off they went behind the girls, who were talking and giggling at everything, but with the distance it could not be heard.

Shawn took a short –cut with Vivek following so that they were in front of the girls, but still a little far.

Shawn closed his eyes and like a blind man felt his way.

Shawn – "Are they close enough to see me, Vivek "?

Vivek- "Yes, quite close ".

Shawn went straight into an electric pole at the side of the road, banged hard, so it seemed and fell straight on the road. Vivek ran for him and so did the four girls.

One ran for water, another put his head on her lap, while Vivek and the other two girls tried to make Shawn comfortable. They sprinkled little water on his face, and as one of them used her handkerchief on his face, Shawn burst out laughing.

The girls would have kicked his back-side with their stilletoes but they also couldn't contain themselves and burst out laughing.

17

Boy Meets Girl

All the boys and girls were sitting waiting for the lecturer to arrive in the class- more of an auditorium. I think, I saw the lecturer inching his way to our class because of a lady-lecturer talking with him. He's such a nice chap – he can't back out from a lady's grasp, whispered the funny boy of the class. Everybody took his talk with a pinch of salt. Another joker from the class "where is this pinch of salt, that I'm looking for? Has anyone brought it to the class?" There was laughter ripping through everyone.

Shawn was sitting right in the middle trying to make caricatures of all the girls scattered here and there. Then his eye caught the eye of a girl looking at him and then onto a paper in front. She was also drawing cartoons of all the boys, like him. He always sat on pins and needles and jumped up to ascertain facts from the girl. Poor fellow, must be full of pins and needles on his pants. Who helped him take them out? Indeed it is a pj.

Shawn – (close to the girl)- "Sweetie, any problem? Do I look cock-eyed?"

Pankhuri- "First my name is Pankhuri and not Sweetie. Second, don't get swollen up, if I tell you that you are handsome and no cock will ever sacrifice his life to gift his precious eyes to you. How will it eye the Red-rooster or the black hen or the white leg-horn?"

Shawn-"Ha, ha ! I like your sense of humour. Did you tickle your funny bone but why were you eyeing me the way you did?"

Pankhuri – " I'm Pankhuri and ---- "

Shawn- "First time I heard it but I will etch it on my chest – never to forget it. "

Pankhuri – "I saw you drawing my caricature and so I retaliated drawing yours. Want to see your cock-eyed face?" Both held hands and laughed and then the lecturer made his entry to cut short their idle gossip.

Shawn was impeccably dressed the next day when Pankhuri with impeccable manners walked in with her friend. She gave him such a sugary look that he wondered what he'll put for his coffee. He found it impossible to dab in such a frivolous topic for 'strength of materials' showed up with glaring questions that he loved to solve and then there were models of buildings to do and Engineering drawing that he had mastered. It was almost 3pm when the proffessors and lecturers called it a day. Pankhuri was languidly walking away when Shawn caught sight of her and ran upto her asking, "Can I have the pleasure of having a cup of tea or coffee with you?"

It looked she was waiting for him to ask her for tea but the outside show was so different.

The college provided a lovely neat and clean cafeteria and everything sold in it was on 'no profit, no loss' basis.

They ordered for two cups of scalding hot coffee and two chicken hamburgers and as they sipped the coffee four eyes melted into each other and the hands that came forward to stealthily grasp the other two shivered with sheer excitement but strayed far away from each other.It was love at first sight of two legs of a boy's trousers and for Shawn the billowing frock just wanted to encompass him and make him a prisoner for life.It was love at first sight or would the reaction been the same had another boy or girl met. The lovely surrounding played it's part and the absence of the biggest deterrent in life, your very own loving parents especially the one who is fragile and has a say in everything and her word is law. Got any idea? Have I given enough clues to bring you closer to the answer? Yes, yes you are very close but not ans-swer but it is anser(yes, that's how we pronounce it, AAN-SER and the W is silent mercifully here, unlike the fat woman, MOM, we love and pine for and hold closest to our heart till this other one comes to make a replacement and who in this world would like to be replaced and hence detested. Yes, normally wives are detested till they prove their love for the mother-in-law and girl-friends very few parents are aware of, till a bump on the stomach tells their son is playing foot-ball with her and time is up to get married.

They, they who? Sorry, my gaze shifted to the other couple on the next table. The story would have taken another twist but for your timely reminder. Forgive me, I'm as human as any of you and my mind waivers as my eyes gloat on anything that GOD has made for admiring. Anyway, we were on Pankhuri and Shawn's table and attending on them like a waiter. Don't get shocked when I tell the truth that an author is a waiter attending on people.

Pankhuri and Shawn had not touched the hamburgers and the chicken inside died more of Axyphyxia than the teeth tearing it apart and the molars munching it to pulp. Hand in hand, so they thought- it was a case of euphoria- they walked to their hostel, six inches above the ground. Anyone in love cannot walk but just fly or float.

That night as Pankhuri lay on her bed to sleep, she could see the dashing, smart Shawn, all hers. A shiver ran down her spine when she loathingly realized she had not even grazed his hand by mistake, leave alone holding it to her heart's content. She started with his shoes and with the shine on it she could see her own reflection. A lovely crease adorned his black pant and the white shirt made him look a thorough gentleman as would a German shepherd with antecedents of his pedigree written in bold ink, brought from Germany as though his character certificate is written on it and he is without a blemish seeing his pure red blood. I have seen owners taking such precious dogs on a leash with so much pride and talking and showing off to all and sundry about it. Sadly their wives look on for they had not uttered a word of praise for their wisdom or how caring she was. 'Go to the dogs' should be these wives' retort. He is already going, what more, my dear? What these dogs keep coming into a man's life and jiggering it. Leave dogs alone or as a love –bite it could give rabies as a birthday present.

Pankhuri was still scrutinizing Shawn for his big, black compassionate eyes and the dark brown hair added charm to his fair looking face. Her lips quivered as she bent forward to kiss his red lips. It was a mirage like an Arab sees an oasis in the Sahara desert in Africa, the biggest desert in the world. The Arab has to live with this illusion for life and she has to live with this illusion till one day it becomes a reality and Shawn hers forever. She thanked God for throwing such a sweet, handsome boy in her lap for goods. (forever).

Shawn forced himself to lie down to think about her, that night. He just saw her smiling face and nothing more. He was intensely happy that he had found her and that she was his.

It was dawn when the Sun just sprinkled it's light in their respective rooms to shake them from their dreams. It was like a stone being thrown into a pond and the circular ripples it forms, is like waking up from your dreams." Get up Shawn and see the sparrows chirping and the doves cooing. The crow is already in my balcony eating crumbs and broken left-over biscuits for break-fast. Wish I could give him a cup of tea to make it a complete breakfast. Every morning, for all these years he comes waking me with his caw-caw," his neighbour, Amit Tiwari, a final year student drawled in his peculiar voice, coming more from his nose than his big mouth. Shawn -"Yes Amit, I'm very much awake." The ragging 'sir' was very conspicuous with it's absence.

Amit – "During last term exam, did you enjoy the potato chips and coffee at 2 in the early morning? Nowhere in India will you find it so cheap and over-loaded in the quarter-plates."

Shawn – " I was really shocked to see the price and we all ate two-two plates, greedy that we are. This idea of 'snacks on wheels' in a hostel is reminiscent of 'Meals on Wheels' on the railway stations. "

18

THE SPOILSPORT

After classes as usual, Shawn took Pankhuri accompanied by her friend, Aarti, who was very keen to meet him. Shawn cursed Pankhuri from inside.(He used the most appropriate hindi one only for his lovely readers to hear- 'Kawab mein Haddi') Fortunately nothing was spilt out for Pankhuri or Aarti to hear otherwise besides Shawn, the author, your friend would both disappear- such is her fury, we adore. Shawn had wanted Pankhuri to pour her sweet-nothings in his ears while she nibbled at them. He liked her to do that. Sitting at the dining table, at home, if he ever got that succulent ear-bone in mutton, he would relish it the most. In front of a lady a man is a real goat (ask any man, including the biggest goat, sitting writing this for you and me- ha,ha) and if he allows the lady to chew on his ears there is nothing alarming. ha, ha. I put these ' ha, ha, ho, ho, ' so that my lovely readers know when to tickle their funny bone, chuckle, giggle or even sneer at the appropriate time so that nobody points an accusing finger that you have not understood what you are reading. Don't you see the television when the back-ground music is laughter and the audience has to join in. This is also done to save the audience's reputation so that he is not caught napping or while seeing an English serial, of which we all are so fond of because of their explicit scenes, that he is following word by word and enjoying. Thank you so much Telly people, Directors for being so kind and showing how learned we are to understand the intricacies of the scenes.

Shawn (he decides to teach Pankhuri a lesson for spoiling his day) "What did you say your name was?"

Aarti – "Pankhuri never introduced me and that is the reason you do not know. Anyway, my name is Aarti and I'm from Mysore."

Shawn –"Show me Aarti, where you got the sore and where and how did you get hurt? Can I take Pankhuri's Aarti? " (a ritual)

Pankhuri (slightly agitated)- "Now Shawn enough of your p.j's?"

Shawn – "Aarti you got bewitching eyes. Anyone sees them once can't help getting attracted to them like a magnet. "

Pankhuri- "I don't think Aarti is getting amused with your imagination and words. I think she's feeling too shy."

Aarti – "No, no I'm not one bit shy but I'm wondering if I'm so pretty, why no boy has ever come so close to tell me about my gazelle eyes? Don't all girls wait to hear such words pouring out of a handsome boy, like Shawn?"

Shawn- "When did I turn myself upside down for all these words to pour out? Did I?"

Pankhuri- "Oh Aarti ! You wanted to finish your 'tutorial work, didn't you?"

Aarti – "Yes, that maybe, but with Shawn around it can wait."

Seeing Pankhuri's oval, gazelle eyed face getting longer, both Shawn and Aarti (who understood he was pulling Pankhuri's legs) gave in, for repercussions to follow would be dangerous to handle. Clever boy to give in before the situation becomes boisterous –lesser for a girl, who can walk out of your life and for a wife who can walk on you till you wish you were dead rather than hear her screeching words in and out of any dictionary. She becomes a tigress ready to maul anyone, not with her teeth but with a weapon called 'tongue lashing' and yet she's the best a man can ever get. Happy, my girls!

Aarti- " I really have to go and Shawn it was lovely meeting you. Pankhuri, you are so lucky to have him but if anytime, you get tired of him or have had enough of him, I'm ready to take over."

With a wink in her eyes, Aarti ran before Pankhuri could hammer her.

Pankhuri – "You, Mr. Shawn, you see any pretty girl and your feet wobbles. Your eyes get fixed on her and your stinking mouth dribbles like an old man."

Shawn- "Okay, okay, let me see your pretty face and see if my mouth really stinks?"

Both cling and squeeze each other, unmindful of the passing people and fortunately there were none to harmlessly oogle at them.

Both ran their fingers on their heads to settle the ruffled hair, which had turned in all directions to, maybe, keep a watch of impending danger like the parents etc and tidy their clothes.

Shawn- "Will you always love me like my dad loves my mother?"

Pankhuri – "Why do you ever doubt me? Even if a prince comes my way, I'll jerk his hands to be in yours forever. You say your dad loves your mom too much. Will you love me the same way all our lives after our formative years in college?"

Shawn- "My dad doesn't go out without my mother, except when he goes out to work."

Pankhuri – "Doesn't your mother ever visit your grand-parents? "

Shawn- "Nor my mother, nor my father have any relatives, atleast I do not know of anyone."

PANKHURI – "How very surprising, even my mom and dad have no one to call their own. Only my mom is very possessive of my dad. Won't allow him to budge to see his friends, till she is going along or they come home. I think they are just crazy over each other. Most of the people consider the word 'possessive' bad but I feel the ones who are head over heels in love (what sort of humans are these, who have their head over the heel- I thought everyone has a head on their shoulder.) Will someone has this trait - 'Give me space, give me space' is something only the so called modern people align to. As long as their needs are fulfilled they want to be far from their partners who they claim, they cannot live without. Their love fades away in 3-4 years, as statistics of divorces will tell you. Their love is just a pretence in a garb few can understand and is just a sham. In the humdrum of life everything is not a bed or bouquet of roses. Roses have thorns; life has innumerable of them.

Shawn- "Okay, okay I would love to be pampered by a doting wife who would always be at my beck and call. I'm not a misogynist (who hates women) not to get married. By the way does your mom trust your dad and does your dad trust your mom? This could also lead to possessiveness or is there a hidden secret that your mom and dad have not shared with you?"

Pankhuri- "I think the same applies for your mom and dad."

Shawn- "Ofcourse, this applies to both our mom and dad and such things cannot be hidden for life. One day they will come out in the open and then both of us can have a good laugh. Let's not be 'kill joys' with such articulate speeches that our love percolates down and turns into black coffee."

Both Shawn and Pankhuri in one accord- "I think our taste –buds are savouring the smell of caffe latte (hot milky coffee) Why don't we go for it? Hurrah, Hurrah."

The cafeteria was buzzing with boys and girls, many in groups in the middle and just as many with girl-friends in the far isolated corners. Shawn and Pankhuri also settled in a remote corner. The crow came 'cawing' on a table just vacated for left-over crumbs before the waiter could lift and clear the table. The squirrels lifted their tails in succession as though it was the Mexican Wave they were performing at a Foot-ball match – perhaps humans learnt it from them-who is to know. The squirrels would grab pieces of bread from the hamburgers thrown by some boys and girls and run to the safety of the trunk of a tree.

Shawn – "See how he is stealing a kiss from his girl-friend?"

Pankhuri- "Then why don't you call the police? He is a thief. Ho ho. "

Shawn- "I like that. I love my girl to be cheerful and cracking jokes."

Pankhuri- "So, she has become a hammer now? He,he,ho,ho. Tell me Shawn which nut behind the wheel has the most accidents?"

Shawn-(knows the answer but wants her happy) "I think walnut."

Pankhuri- "You, my dear. Ha, ha" (Feeling very happy that she had won him, but he was happier that he could make her laugh) Such is love when you can sacrifice anything for your girl-friend to see a streak of laughter or smile on her face and a smile is a silent laugh. Once you are married and children come in, then your love is diverted and you start sleeping with the enemy.(wife)

Most of the seats were empty and if you had ears long enough, you could hear the chairs heaving a sigh of relief

"Work is done for the day" she whispers to the table and we'll have a lovely time the night through enacting what we learnt the whole day from these boys and girls.

Table- "Sweetheart, can you tell me where your mouth is?"

Chair- "I'm also trying to ascertain where my mouth is. I even asked the bench but she herself wants to know which side is her head and which side is her tail. Poor humans are not developed enough to hear all our frequencies except the creaking one or else they would be eaves-dropping or put CCTV cameras for surveillance."

Both Shawn and Pankhuri jumped up to go.

When they reached her hostel gate, she waved him 'sweet dreams' and a flying kiss. He saw her walking with the gait of a model as she vanished through the gate. Gates are really magicians, who welcome all and sundry with their rusty throats which has turned hoarse because of lack of machine oil, for those who go in just disappear from the one who came to leave them.

19

LIFE IN THE COLLEGE

Shawn closed the back door of his room while the front door lay wide open, as was usual with all the boys. He sat down at his table with books spread all over it.

A boy Sujoy Dutta from the same floor- "Can I take your Maths reference book that you brought from the Library?" Shawn –"Anything to ask? Just take it."

Sujoy – "Thanks yaar. Were you there when the cobra snake came out in the dining hall?"

Shawn –"No yaar, what happened?"

Sujoy- "We were all sitting enjoying our food when one of the workers ran out of the store room with a cobra following. It seems the snake and the worker got scared of each other, the snake did not tell but the worker did, later.

The worker ran out banging the main dining room door with the slithery reptile still following, trying to escape. It slid through the door and into the small front drain covered with a slab of stone. The boys ran behind trying to pull it out but all effort was in vain and futile. You know, I'm scared of snakes so I kept a distance but was inquisitive to know the outcome. The boys burnt paper, cloth soaked in kerosene oil but it refused to leave the ensconced safety of the drain.

Then Raghubir, the final year boy just lifted the stone slab. Imagine, he put his hand under the slab; the snake could have bitten him but he is so brave. He is a real hero, I must say. He killed the snake with an iron rod that was lying close by.

The illiterate workers burnt it saying it has clicked their photographs with it's eyes and it's partner would come looking for them to take revenge."

Shawn- "Oh, I missed it –must have been fun."

Sujoy – "Okay Shawn, see you in the morning. Good-night, sorry, good morning."

Shawn dived back into his books. He still had to complete part of the model he was assigned to do. It was almost 1.30 a.m when he got up to stretch himself like a cat. Had anyone been watching him they would have heard the purring noise also.

Shawn lay down to sleep but his eyes refused to close. He coaxed his eye-lids to shut so that he could visualize his sweet-heart, Pankhuri. He thought more and dreamt less. He saw in his mind's eye, Pankhuri in her night dress, pouring over her books and seeing his photograph placed safely in between the pages of her book. The pages held him tight, so much so that he got suffocated- he would have loved to be breathless in her arms. What he never knew that Pankhuri with her friends was playing table –tennis in the common room of her hostel to divert her attention from Shawn's thoughts. She failed in her attempt so she picked up her mobile and rang him. He was delighted to hear her soft voice and merged his with so many adjectives for her that Grammar became so easy like reading the back of her hand.

Pankhuri- "I phoned to wish you bye for the night."

Shawn – "Bye, till we meet in the morning."

Pankhuri- "Bye once again" and hung up.

Shawn cursed himself for agreeing to say 'bye' so soon. He abused himself again and again with all the dozen abuses he knew till he could picture her no more for he was snoring.

20

Romance On The Cards

Shawn – "What if your parents insist on you marrying a doctor?"

Pankhuri- "I'll start eating apples from today – an apple a day keeps the --------"

Shawn –"Doctor away and Shawn to stay."

Pankhuri – "Do all lovers become poets?"

Shawn – "Yes, as long as any strain of love remains."

Pankhuri – "And after that?"

Shawn- "They are kicked by their loving wives to go and earn, even pull a rickshaw? Whew, let's go."

Pankhuri – "What brainwaves you get suddenly."

Shawn to Pankhuri – "Jump up my fat lump of sugary pie."

Pankhuri –"You called me fat. I'll starve till I become a skeleton and your kisses can thrive on the bone marrow."

Shawn – "What rubbish I'll enjoy bone soup, especially your funny bone. Ha,ha,ho,ho,he,he.

Pankhuri – "Okay, tickle my funny bone."

Shawn – A pleasantly plump lady, had a lovely Persian purring cat who sat on the Persian carpet lapping her favourite chicken soup everyday.

One day the lady by mistake, instead of chicken soup served petrol in the bowl.

The cat just lapped it up without even opening her eyes to see what she was having.

Then she ran right round the building once, twice, thrice four times, fifth time, sixth time, seventh time, eighth time, ninth time tenth time and then fell flat on the ground."

Pankhuri – "What happened?"

Shawn- "Just ran out of petrol. Ha,ha.

Pankhuri – "You repeat such ancient jokes that only a pre-historic man can laugh."

Shawn – "Okay, ok, modern lady let's get going, as he pulled her with him."

They walked to an outside 'dhaba' (usually a poor man's

Restaurant) where everyone knew all the boys and girls of the college who sat dunking (dipping biscuits in the tea and eating) biscuits in their tea to have it.

Shawn – Calling a friendly rickshawala, "Ramu o' Ramu, give me your rickshaw, (as he put Rs 20/ in his palms) go have tea and biscuits while I give my lady a ride."

Ramu – "Arre sahib, this is not for you. You come sit and I'll take you both."

On Shawn's persistence he let go with a laugh "you can't ride it, sir."

In her lady-like way, Pankhuri climbed the rickshaw. Shawn jumped on to the rickshawala's seat and started pedaling.

"Chalo market rickshawala" exulted Pankhuri in her effervescent (bubbly) and eloquent voice.

Shawn found the rickshaw going side-ways, leaving the tarred road. "How do they manage it?" he thought and after a lot of struggle brought it back on the road like an unwilling naughty boy brought back to school.

"Hurrah, hurrah "they regaled every passerby who looked at them with bleary eyes and dabbled back in their own eccentric ways with "Yeh boy "

Shawn found quite a task to turn back. Fortunately, a round-about stood in front to come to his rescue. Shawn felt it was GOD_SENT and was all praises for the ALMIGHTY. There was quite a gathering at the dhaba and an upheaval at their arrival with claps unleashing from the palms of everyone present. The rickshawala was the most excited to see a 'saheb' gracing his rickshaw.

Shawn and Pankhuri could carry such memories for life and dip into it for enjoyment and happiness and thrill all their friends with such a tale.

21

Shawn's Mom Visits Assam

The festival of lights, Diwali or Deepawali, was at hand and everybody was looking forward to go home. Any festival, whether Eid, Christmas, Baisakhi etc etc, unites the near and dear ones. Shawn and Pankhuri were not happy going home and leaving each other. This is one thing every lover detests but if wishes were horses, beggars would ride. I don't wish to enact a scene where tears flow freely. Detest as I would, but our world is so full of unhappiness that miseries and salt water from human emotions do seep and creep in most impenetrable places.

India has very less places of entertainment. The two Movie and parks have become inaccessible to most of the poor people for the in exorbitant tickets in the malls. The other one the parks have put tickets for entry. A poor family cannot make both ends meet.

Sunny- "Mama, take us to the garden today?"

Phoolwati- "Beta, they have put Rs 5/head for entry to the garden, how can we pay so much money just for entry for five people and then you want chips etc. Forget how we used to go earlier, every now and then but now with your dad's meagre salary how can we manage? This world is not for the poor. The rich uncles sitting managing the garden and park will never understand the woes of the poor.

Sunny- "But mama, weren't the parks made for the children to play in free, then how come these uncles are making us pay? Are they anti the poor or against the children? "

Such small talk abounds everywhere in India and maybe in other poor nations but who is there to heed or even think of the poor? Who am I 'a nitwit ' to draw peoples' ire when GOD above is enjoying the show HE created.

Phoolwati- "Beta, I read 'Thakur Saheb ka Kua' by Prem Chand written in Hindi. The poor man could not get even clean water from the rich man's compound to drink. These rich people are still the same.

Pankhuri – "Shawn why don't you call your mum and dad to Assam to spend the Diwali holidays with my parents?"

Shawn – "Oh, that would be a lovely idea for us to be together, but won't it be easier for two (your dad and mom) to travel to Delhi rather than four to travel to Assam?"

Pankhuri- "I have no objection for that also, my lord. I was just thinking of holding your hands in Darjeeling and walking or going to Cherrapunji, with the highest rainfall in the world, and sing 'Tu,tu,tu,tu meri-ri,ri,ma tera hone laga ' in the rain.' What days it will be, I just can't resist. Get your parents to say 'yes', please sweet-heart. "Amid fears, and hoping their children had made the right choice, both parents agreed that Shawn's parents, Pankhuri and Shawn will fly to Assam.

On the day of the flight, Shawn's father had a very important meeting and had to cancel his ticket. However, he forced Shawn's unwilling mother to go, for he himself would be out of the city.

There was an instant rapport between Shawn's mother and Pankhuri's father as they cuddled and huddled together for tea.

Pankhuri – "Where is mom and where is my little brother, dad?"

Pankhuri's dad –"Your mom had to go for your brother's admission to Mumbai and made me stay for you all.

Pankhuri – " It would have been so nice, if Shawn's papa had to come along but so sweet of him to send Shawn's mom. Wish my mom was also here and my lazy brother. Has Munnu really become so big to go out and look after himself?"

Shawn's mother – "What a dahling your daughter is?" and was lost, for maybe a second, but all noticed her.

Pankhuri – "Any problems maa? Anything amiss?"

Shawn's mother – "I was just thinking Shawn is so lucky to have such a pretty girl, so full of manners and so much love and care for the elderly."

Mr Jhunjhunwala (Pankhuri's dad)- "I think I can reciprocate that your son, Shawn, will look after my daughter very well. I think both are well met and I put my seal of approval for him to be my son-in-law. Even Pankhuri's mother would have readily agreed with my thinking. How I wish she was here."

Normally, a wife is like salt. You do not know her value except when she is not with you and a mother is remembered only when you see an old rocking chair.

Mr Jhunjhunwala (Pankhuri's father) – "What would you like for break-fast, Shawn and what does your mother like? Anybody needs sugar-free for diabetes?"

Pankhuri – "Since when did you start worrying about food dad? And am I not here to see to it? Just relax and be your usual self." She could sense the queasy (worried) look on his face, with mum not there but when she looked around she found, typical of her mother, everything in place and in abundance.

Pankhuri's dad –"Okay, okay the little mother is here to look after everything. Should I start with an old pilfered (stolen) joke I read ages back, Shawn?"

Mrs Sheila Singh (Shawn's mother) –"Oh, it will be wonderful, old or new. "

Shawn was so close to Pankhuri and yet so far as long as the old man remained in his vicinity. "Can't they keep to themselves and leave the young ones alone. Have they forgotten their own days?" he whispered to himself and out of reach of their hearing.

Shawn- Crack the joke uncle, like we crack a boiled egg,"

Hoping Pankhuri's dad would forget the joke though he liked him a lot but Mr Jhunjhunwala was firm as a rock and showed no signs of forgetting what he was about to say.

Pankhuri Jhunjhunwala's father- "A Chinese and an Indian went to the grave-yard."

Much to the Indian's consternation (surprise) the Chinese offered rice while the Indian put flowers on the grave.

The Indian could not contain himself and asked the Chinese "When do you expect your man to come and eat the rice?"

Chinese – "Why, at the same time yours comes and smells the flowers?"

The joke was reminiscent of Akbar (King- Mughal Dynasty) and Birbal's time but palatable out of respect and it was, without a doubt, humorous or to placate (please) the old man or his inimitable style or was it, he was going to be his father-in-law- most likely the last.

There was a lot of cacophony of giggles and loud laughter. Shawn's hand, unawares to everyone or so he thought for love is blind (If love is blind how did he find her tresses – No logic, my lord- ha,ha) quietly pulled Pankhuri's tresses (hair) to entwine his manly fingers onto her nimble and delicious ones. Delicious because everyone big enough must have watched with interest lovers holding hands or chewing on them, surely must be tasty.

Mr Jhunjhunwala (Pankhuri's dad) was in his element again. Was he ringing his Jhunjhuna (toy) – just pulling his legs. Did he have a peg? Pankhuri's mom was not there to nudge and stop him from drinking, for alcohol doesn't listen to the pleas of men for it flows like all liquids in gutters of men with least resistance and who don't put dykes like Holland to stop the flow. (of seas).

God made the earth a hexagon (with six sides) and said "In every corner, men will find good and loving wives, but with time the corners got rubbed out and the earth took it's present round shape, and thus the evil cities of Sodom and Gomorrah were born with no good wives left.

Some understood the joke, others put up a pretense to show their gray matter, but all went wild with laughter.

There was a general outcry for Shawn to crack joke especially from Pankhuri.

Shawn –"I have no hammer to crack jokes and then everyone has heard most of them. Fresh ones from the oven have yet to arrive." Instead he came out with what was uppermost in his thoughts.

He started on a funny note for others but not for himself.

"If you obey all the rules in school you miss out all the fun when the teacher has her back to you, writing on the board and chalks flying all over.

Later in life, you still follow the rules then again you miss out the 'miss' who would have been your wife but today is your friend's wife.

Now, if you wake up to shake and break the rules, you are shaking yourself- too old to enjoy the fun.

So, it all boils down to – enjoy when you can and to hell with the rules.

Everyone was aghast with his knowledge that all acquire only in old age.

Shawn's mom – Mrs Sheila Singh- "If your dad was here he would have been very proud of you, my son.

Pankhuri - "Aunty show us uncle's photograph?"

Mrs. Sheila Singh (Shawn's mother) – Shawn bring my purse. Your dad's photo is always there."

Shawn brought the purse and his mother took out the photograph and gave it to Pankhuri.

Pankhuri – "Shawn what a handsome dad you have and you are an exact replica of him. See dad how, how sweet. Dad, almost never saw the photo properly, but grudgingly admired it and returned it. No man, as ugly or handsome believed to be from Mars rotating anti-clockwise or any lady supposed to be from Venus rotating clock-wise would ever confide that another man or lady is very handsome or very pretty.

While both her father and his mother were busy talking, Shawn desperately tried to attract Pankhuri's attention but she was still looking at the photograph and trying to recollect something.

Shawn – "Any problem with the photograph? "

Pankhuri - "Such photos are not to be shown to everybody or else they'll want the owner of the photo for themselves. I'll not show yours to anyone – can't say whose eyes get attracted to you and I can't afford to lose you - such a sweetheart."

Just then Mr Singh 's mobile rang. "Hullo son, how is the weather there?"

Shawn- "It's not Cherrapunji, but it's raining cats and dogs here."

Dad (Mr Singh) – Bring some German Shepherds, Alsatians, pugs and Dalmatians. We can open a shop. They are going quite expensive here and free there. (raining).

22

A RICKSHAW –PULLER'S LIFE

Every good thing must come to an end. I must add here, so also the bad.

Shawn's mother had gone back happy as a lark to get a daughter-in-law as sweet as Pankhuri. She had made inroads into Pankhuri's life and with the gift of the gab that she was endowed with, she made tales after tales to tell Shawn's father till his ears nearly fell off. How did he hear then and what did she do with the crispy ears? Cooked them?

In the beginning the dream come true about his son's happiness was really welcome, but the repetition and chewing the cud (was she a Buffalo?) made him very uneasy.

Mr Singh (Shawn's dad) – "Why did you come back so soon?"

Shawn's mum- "After marriage I have stuck to you like a stamp on an addressed envelope, like a leech. Mainly, I couldn't stay without you and you know friends and fish stink after two days."

Shawn's dad- "I was wondering where the stink was coming from."(Giggles)

Shawn's mum- "Till Pankhuri and Shawn are married, we cannot thrust ourselves on them. Anyway, Shawn has made a lovely choice and he should be very, very happily married and we'll have grand-children to play with soon. Shawn's final year is nearing completion. Already he has been offered jobs. Both families can meet and chalk out a date for the marriage. I'm going to wear ---------"

Shawn's father cut her short with "Okay, okay we'll see.

He felt the urgency very sinister looking in such a delicate matter as marriage.

Shawn's mother – "In my wildest dreams I could not have got such a nice girl like Pankhuri, for Shawn. Pankhuri's father, mother like us make such a nice pair though I saw the mother only in the photograph. What fun Pankhuri and I had coming back from the market in a rickshaw. The rickshaw puller's pant was all torn and tattered in the wrong places, with butcher's stitches which hid less and showed more. To pull us both on a slope he would leave his seat to get more leverage.

Pankhuri – Amidst giggles," did you see his BUMS aunty?" She spelt it so that he had no inkling we were talking about him and that too in English.

Shawn's mother - "Ya, dirty black ones. See, see even his U- N- D- E- R W-E-A-R has got H-O-L-E-S."

Pankhuri – "Poor chap".

Shawn's mother –Mrs Singh- "Not poor. What they earn day to day they won't buy clothes but will spend 1/3 rd on a pint of the rice brew (liquor). For their wives they keep kicks ready when they ask for money and send their children loitering and begging for alms."

He was huffing and puffing like an engine when we were almost on our door-step. Pankhuri handed him the money as they got down from the rickshaw.

Rickshaw Puller (in chaste English) "Thank you ma'am for the money and thanks for all the compliments about my torn and tattered pant. I,m a graduate without a job, as are so many of us. I can't make both ends meet so I did not get married to the girl I loved and I'm only sun-burnt. Poor people like us hear your giggles everyday but we have become immune to ----------------------" He was still talking when we were running towards our gate, with tears in our eyes out of shame. Do the poor only have to get the butt end of everything bad. I still stand confirmed this world is not made for the poor- it is a rich man's bastion.

23

IS SOMETHING AMISS

'Twenty braying donkeys do not a single neighing horse make ' was rubbed into us by both our teachers and our parents right from childhood.

It would take countless comedians to take the anger out of our Nation, to enjoy our short lived lives of 70-80 years by tickling our funny bones.

Why can't we all remember that we are children of God and made of the same flesh and blood to enjoy this lovely life and then when our time is up nobody can revive us, not even the doctors or the piles of money that we have accumulated, most likely with debauchery. There is no escape, my dear boys, from the clutches of death. Then who is there who can help mankind? My lovely, delicate, doe eyed girls. Yes, the mother who tells her son and husband not to go out and fight. Then the slender, newly married girl, the one who absorbs your life who tells you, you have to live for her and for the children who are to arrive soon. Come on you soft-hearted girls, mother and wife included, rein your husband and son with the rain of love that they never go out and fight. Now tell me, where the heated arguments and the fisticuffs that follow, have vanished. GIVE IT A TRY. It may take sometime for things to drift our way and then there will be only happiness.

Now, don't stop reading the novel for the small advice that I have given.

T'ring, t'ring, t'ring Shawn's mother picked up the unrelenting landline phone singing it's own tune.

"Hullo, who is the sweet-heart on the other end with such a suave, rassogulla voice?"

From the other end – "Am I talking to the robber, who is out to snatch my daughter, Pankhuri?"

Shawn's mother – "For a second, I really missed my heart-beat. Yes, I'm the snatcher, Shawn's mom. I really missed you when we came last month to your place. Has your son got admission in the college? It would have been so nice holding hands and hearing your sweet voice pouring all the news of your place into my bat ears?."

Pankhuri's mother – Don't worry, you can hear all the gossip when we come next month to fix up the date to get Shawn and Pankhuri knotted up in marriage. Shawn's father and I will, most probably com -----"

Shawn's mother who is a fast thinker – "So- so, sorry, very sorry, already we have booked our tickets for next month to come to Assam. We had planned it as a surprise to you. It would have been so pathetic with two trains crossing each other in opposite directions taking people further away, who wanted to meet. Would have enjoyed breaking each other's locks to get into their houses and neighbours phoning for the police. Nice time to get all the secrets of the house when the owners are not there."

Pankhuri's mother - "I think it applies to your house also, when we ransack your house to get all the truths and secrets of the Singhs. What songs they sing. And when we meet in person, it will be such a blast. I'm just waiting to meet and what a lovely surprise, indeed I'll tell Pankhuri's dad to cancel the tickets. So you both are coming. It'll be fun to have you both here. Come, most welcome." She hung up.

Shawn's dad who heard traces of the talk since he was in and out of the room, doing some house-hold chores, was surprised to see such an accommodating wife not wanting guests and that too Pankhuri's mum and dad and asked- "When did we book our tickets for Assam or you wanted to give me a surprise too?"

Shawn's mom- "See our house needs a little colour – washing. They will come here for the first time and I want to show them a sparkling house. That is why I did not want them to come now and nobody will come enquiring if we really booked the tickets or not and they do not doubt my words.

Shawn's dad slightly shaken up with her lies, could not believe his ears. Certainly she never behaved like this before. "I really take my hat off for your fast thinking. Had I been in your place, I would have stuttered and come out with 'most welcome anytime' and he caught and squeezed her tight "Just you wait, tonight. It's so nice to be all alone, like when we just got married and on our honey-moon but I still miss my children."

Shawn's mother - "You mean Shawn, he's a child not children and you have closed my mouth not to speak and when I wanted more children, you wouldn't have it. How I yearned for ---- kids but you said no. How did Shawn suddenly spring into our intimacy as usual. Soon he will be married and won't look at you. "

Shawn's father – "He's our son and I know my blood doesn't forget so easily."

Shawn's mother (little upset) – "Okay, okay, I believe you but is your trumpeter dead that you have to blow your own bugle to announce the colour of your blood."

Shawn's father – "Someone has to learn to talk from you but I know how to put a stop to it, as he gathered her once again in his arms and stopped all her talk with a tight kiss and through the chinks in his mouth in inaudible tone, the night can wait but I can't. "

Shawn's mother - "Your love is the only thing that has stood by me, that I have not opened my mo------" and then, once again, his grip on her mouth tightened.

24

Inexplicable- What To Make Of It.

Shawn was busy with the models – not the ones on the stilettoes and with a walk that erodes even the very innocent if by chance somebody takes them along. It was the architectural models that he was designing late in the night along with his friends.

Aftab – " Shawn, if we conceive this building's design the way sir felt and explained won't it be like any other ordinary skyscraper?"

Prabhu – " Yes, of course we are different and our expertise in designing, as sir says, is immaculate and we have to keep to our name. "

Shawn – "I hate to be an ordinary architect (R-KEY-TECT) who take out their cars early morning and with their mobiles keep clicking different buildings, just to incorporate those designs in their buildings with a slight twist here or a slight twist there. I hate copy-cats and hate to be one. Okay, okay let's get going - an idea just struck me. Let's give it a try.

All three, pooled their heads in to come to some understanding and found the design would be an instant hit with a few modifications.

Aftab - "Will this be able to bear the tensile stress? Check how much you calculated Shawn and Prabhu yours was differing slightly.

Shawn picked up his exercise copy to check the readings while Prabhu waded through all the modeling paper and other sticking material to search for his exercise copy on which he had done the calculation. He just couldn't find it amongst so much strewn paper. Instead he came across a little tuft of hair and on pulling it further found it was artificial black hair, nice and long for a girl. " Now, who on earth, is using this girl's hair?" as he tried to put it on top of his unkempt hair.

Shawn – "Don't go out with that hair on your head or else some boys will be running after you. You look soo sweet. "

Prabhu – "Let me try on you, Aftab" and Aftab very willingly put his head forward as though a crown awaited the beauty queen. He was also muscular like Shawn but it transformed him into a lady with good looks. Some people might co- relate it to eunuchs but there was no trace of it anywhere.

Shawn – "Stop acting like babies. Throw the damn hair and let's complete our work."

Prabhu – "A-ha, so you don't want to show us your girly looks," as he tried to catch Shawn who tried to evade him by ducking. Aftab came from the side and caught him and then "Go ahead and enjoy your whims and fancies "as Shawn gave his head to be crowned. There was an instant transformation only a salwaar- kameez was lacking for shawn to look like a girl.

Both friends, Aftab and Prabhu, stood wonder-struck, gaping at Shawn as though some miracle or some magic had taken place. Both were unable to explain.

Shawn looked at their whimsical and astonished looks and shouted "What happened?" There was no reply but Prabhu ran to his room and brought his shaving mirror. Shawn looked into the mirror and saw Pankhuri's face in it instead of his own, apart from the stubble that had grown on his handsome, now pretty face.

Long afterwards, late into the morning he kept thinking how such a thing was possible but his inner-voice did not come to his rescue. He thought of the old wives' tales that every person has seven similar faces to their own and took respite from it. He could not restrain himself and even told Pankhuri who laughed it off saying husband and wife look same after some years together and in their case it happened earlier. She even told Shawn's mother who laughed it off and after that it just died a natural death.

25

Bring 'Heaven' Home

Shawn loved his father and mother just as much as Pankhuri loved hers.

Shawn would phone them every night before they slept. He would even narrate something interesting that had happened in the day to keep his parent's spirits high. He felt they were lonely without him. He even told his mother about the girl's hair and what the mirror had to tell but she laughed it off and told Shawn she will tell his father when he comes but there was nothing in it. On another occasion he told them this and asked them to revert with the answer next day.

"When students do wrong and the principal catches them, why do they shiver in their pants?"

The mother had an instant answer "Seeing the principal, ice forms in their pants and so they shiver."

"But mamma when the ice in the pants thaw (melts) then what happens to the trousers?" Shawn enquired.

Shawn's father – "That answer you know very well. Your mother has changed your trousers many, many times when you were young.

Both father and mother had this facility of hearing and talking because the 'loud-speaker' on the land-line phone was on. Such a cordial relationship is very, very rare. The whole family was cloistered together in one big cluster and no outsiders or even neighbours could say they had a cantankerous (fighting) nature. They had hewn (cut) their family in such a happy-go-lucky way that no one could insinuate (point) a finger at them.

Love-birds that they were, both went to the railway station and booked two tickets for Guwahati.

Shawn's dad – Mr. Singh - Two confirmed tickets for Guwahati in 3-tier berths, Rajdhani express for 22nd of next month.

Booking Clerk – "Sorry sir, no berths available for next month in Rajdhani Express. You can avail the confirmed tickets only in Assam Mail."

Mr Singh – "Have the touts bought all the tickets already in advance to sell at a premium."

Booking clerk – "Please sir, there is a big queue waiting and please fill the form."

Men from the back queue started howling- people here just need somebody to excite or ignite the situation and then only reinforcements of police or the army can bring the situation back to normal. They are like sheep – one goes one way, the others are sure to follow without thinking. "This is my 3rd day in this line and everytime my turn comes either there is a lunch break or confirmed tickets not available. This corruption is in all government organizations and that is why to get into any government job you have to pay lacs. This babu (clerk) must have also paid lacs and now he is withdrawing the lost money. Indeed lucrative."

Booking clerk – "When you are aware of everything than why such a hue and cry? You know from top to bottom everyone gets their share, why you blame only the poor babus?"

Shawn's dad – "Okay, okay give me for Assam Mail, handing the filled form to the clerk."

There is a burst of a huge wave crashing but as it approaches the shore it calms down, so also with this jostling crowd who shout their lungs out and then are quiet with no one listening. What the rich and mighty forget if a tsunami of the poor raises it's ugly head, then there will be no one to save them.

'Governments come and governments go but I go on for ever' is a refrain corruption sings.

Shawn's mum – "Why did you book in the 3 tier when you always travel by air or 1st class by train?" – She was on pins and needles to know.

Shawn' s dad – "My dear 3 tier is comparatively safe, whereas 1st class becomes very lonely in these troublesome times."

Mrs Singh – "How clever and thoughtful you can be?" as she squeezed his hand –her right and his left. It was her 'right' to do so and he was not 'left' out of his pleasure.

All the women have this power of bringing Hell or Heaven to a man's hearth. Just antagonize her and let her wrath ebb over and you are extending an invitation to 'Hell with you' or just purr 'yes boss' to your wife and watch 'Heaven' dusting it's feet on the door-mat and gyrating affably to endorse it's presence in that house, 'er home with it's warmth, that never burns.

26

WHAT'S IN A NAME

All the colleges were up in arms - not with sticks and stones to break your bones but with tongue lashing, logically and suavely as though grease was spread on the speaker's palate and sugary sweet words flew as aeroplanes fly from the air-strips.

"Shawn, Shawn my name has appeared in the Annual Meet at Nainital from 25th of this month on the Notice board for the debate on 'What's in a name'. Just check if your name has also appeared for it on your hostel notice," almost screeching in excitement was the voice of Pankhuri on the other end.

"As yet I did not check but I'll do as soon as I can especially when my sweet-heart is going and I'll force myself in even if I have to," whispered a sweet, manly voice of Shawn.

"I won't go if you are not in the list," the crest-fallen voice of Pankhuri answered, putting the phone down.

"Yaar, (friend) why do you trouble her so much, when you know your name has appeared in practically everything. I wish my name was also there or is it the selectors do not know the spelling of Prabhu," laughed his friend loudly sitting in front.

The speaker regaled the crowd with his wit and humour and his extra-ordinary wisdom. He seemed to be abreast of the latest news and threw big enough chocolates for all to suck, seated comfortably in rows to hear the debate, even with answers that were quite remote from the truth.

He asked the crowd of students sitting one side. "What are the three new elements in the periodic table named that were in the news-paper recently?" It was a difficult question though they were engineering students and he was sure there would be no answers. Most of the students wanted to test him instead and asked him for the answer, thinking he may not know. He started to tell but a voice rang out Nihonium (Nh), Moscovium(Mc) and Tennessine (Ts) and there was such a roar of applause that the hall would have collapsed had the speaker not asked for silence. Shawn was called on the stage, for it was he who had unraveled the answer and journalist's cameras were blazing out fire clicking photos for the next days news-paper.

The emcee's words were hammering on people's minds. He turned the tide for the general public and asked the answer to this joke.

"Why you people are not in your element today?"

There was an eerie silence compared to the earlier commotion and then a rustic voice with age and a throat that needed lot of cleaning spoke from amongst the crowd "Because all the elements in the Periodic table have reacted and become compounds." There was a thundering applause to such a lovely answer and the Ha, ha, ho, ho continued for long, unabated.

Peering down on all the crowd, was the banner hanging on four cords with 'WHAT'S IN A NAME 'and asking politely 'arguably yours ' if you win with words justifying what you speak suavely and the Trophy was for your college to keep.

Miss Neelu Chhabra of Nainital college of Nutrition will lead the way in speaking for the motion.

"The honourable judges and my lovely guests will understand that my skirt is not wet with loose motions and yet I speak for the motion. There was an instant rapport with the crowd who went berserk with laughter of appreciation.

Rose with any other name would smell just as sweet." Poor Shakespeare must have rolled in his grave to hear speaker after speaker naming him. Maybe it was, Shakespeare's Day and who had the wit and wisdom to shake his thinking.

Last but not least, we have Pankhuri Jhunjhunwala from Final year of ----------------- and it was lost in the din that the crowd created hearing her name and from Shawn and his friends.

"yes, my honourable Judges, my humourous guests and above all my own friends sitting on pins and needles to see me win, I do carry a 'jhunjhuna' for all of you to play with and enjoy yourself. I am so happy that my name 'Jhunjhunwala 'made you all laugh and I'm sure many blood pressures must have gone down. Where many comedians have failed, my name has amused many. Had my name been any other it would have fallen flat – the crowd here has proved my point that a name has a lot to say.

If you have read the latest book 'I write HE DICTATES- A Love Story' by an unknown author, Arnold Iwin Francis, you will understand during partition of India, Mr Singh would not be hounded in Pakistan if his name was Mr Iqbal. A name would spell Life or Death. True a rose would smell the same as our greatest author, Shakespeare says, with any other name but not so, people. I'm sure, my name has rung in the Judges' ears and they are deftly putting it on the paper and hopefully right on top. Adieu, Sayonara and our students own, 'See You'. "What do you think, I'll see you too". Sorry judges, my honourable ones, this was not for you but for my dear friends. There was such an uproar from the crowd that nothing could be heard except 'Pankhuri, Pankhuri or Jhunjhunwala.

When one of the Judges stood up to speak with paper in hand, everyone shouted in chorus, Pankhuri, Pankhuri and indeed Pankhuri Jhunjhunwala had carried the day with a trophy in hand for her college.

Two eyes were continuously on each other with two hands showing the thums up sign – who else but Shawn and Pankhuri.

27

THE NAME OF THE GAME-FOOTBALL.

Evening drew everyone out on the Soccer field with a foot-ball that all the 22 players from both sides got after. The football was feeling very shy but in very high spirits to see so many people after it. It did feel slightly dejected when they kicked her around but when the goal-keeper held it tight what ecstasies it went through, even I cannot describe.

The referee blew his whistle and the captain of the home team, the Nainital Engineering college, kicked the ball to his left-in and they were off like leopards with a speed of 110km/hour. Shawn was the captain of the other team-The Great Bustard Engineering college and saw the ball quite close to his goal-keeper. He left his position and ran to help the full-back, retrieved the ball and tried to 'carry' it to his team-mate but found no way out and so passed it to his own goal-keeper who missed it and the ball just rolled into the goal at snail-speed with no one to stop it. Within 5 minutes of the game, the Nainital college was jumping with triumph and happiness and victory very much in sight. Their coach was goading them to carry on the massacre and Shawn's coach holding his head in his palms with guilt and shame. The opponent team's morale was right up. Shawn looked at Pankhuri. Girls, normally are a pillar of strength to the boys but found her eyes closed. She was sitting along with the other boys and girls, shouting themselves hoarse.

Shawn took the ball and carried it like a torpedo right next to the mouth of their goal, pushed it to his team-mate to score, who kicked hard but miles away from the target. The score-board still showed 1-0 with impunity and with a sneer, few could comprehend. (understand).

Both sides put their heart and soul in the game but both teams were not ready to concede. One minute the ball was this side and the next moment it was on the other side. Both sides were tough having passed the 'Quarter Final,' Semi-Final and now the Final. The poor foōt-ball had no choice of staying with this team or that- if it liked Shawn's team and wanted to stay with them, their side would certainly loose. Time and again, Shawn made inroads into their side but just stopped short of the rectangle. In a jiffy, the ball had reached their side and precariously hit the goal-post and rebounded where Shawn had reached to help. In the twinkling of an eye he saw Pankhuri and the ball touched his hand. A penalty shot was given and the home-team converted it into a goal. The red score-board glared 2-0 as though making fun of the visitors- look more at the girls and they'll ruin you.

It was almost off-time, when Shawn like a dart carried the ball and into the goal but before the ball entered the goal-post the referee had blown the whistle for Off-time. There was such a hue and cry but he was adamant and possibly he was right for there was a stop-watch to guide him. A goal scored in vain, suggesting all do their work on time.

The home-team coach was thumping the player's back, "Bravo, my boys –you have done it and now nothing can take the sheen off you."

In the other corner, the Bustards were consoled "There is still the 2nd half and I have faith in my boys."

Every nerve, every muscle was taut. Excitement ran high as though climbing mount Everest. Shawn with the speed that he gathered carried the ball as though it was stuck to his feet with some adhesive and passed it on to Aftab who just changed the direction of the ball and into the goal where it got tangled up with the net, which tried to stop it from rolling further into mischievous hands.

The score-board hesitatingly put the score 2-1.

From both sides, there was a lot of resistance, but when the opportunity of a corner came, Shawn just headed the ball in with the goal-keeper fumbling and stumbling after it.

The score-board was neutral and willingly showed 2-2. Did it acquire human qualities staying with them so long?

There was such a tumultuous scene at the stands where clapping would not stop, long after both sides had settled down.

Without money exchanging hands, "I think there will be a tie?" "You bet, Shawn will strike again." shouted another boy sitting next to him and an ardent fan of his. He had hardly finished his sentence when there was a loud cheer, minus the cheer-girls, for One of the players had shot the ball into the goal which hit the goal-post, where Aftab headed it into the goal where their backs headed it out. Shawn saw the opportunity missing and got the ball under his control, zig-zagged three players and the goal-keeper could not thwart the ball from entering the prohibited area –the goal.

Such a chaos of happiness and dejection was on sale for free that people bathed in it and came out refreshed with glowing faces and a tongue that would not stop from chattering like a monkey with praises for Shawn, the hero and his team.

Where was Shawn? Where could he be, except with Pankhuri.

28

JOKES APART

Shawn, Pankhuri and Aftab were sitting in their favourite haunt-the canteen and sipping coffee.

As friendly as you are with anyone, lovers cannot be the same as when they are alone. Here Aftab was in the way and so the best thing to while away the time was idle talk, gossip or jokes.

Pankhuri was the first to break the ice. Did she carry a hammar with her always?

"Tell me the difference between a car, a lady and a donkey? This is a very old joke coming from my parent's time?

Both the boys had not heard of it or had just forgotten. Very few people can remember jokes is an acknowledged fact.

Both sat dumb till Pankhuri gave out the answers.

"A lady is Oh dear! A car is too dear". and then she was quiet.

Shawn could not wait for the last answer and asked "And a donkey?"

Pankhuri was waiting for this opportunity, "You dear! "

"Okay, okay, I'll also ask you a riddle before I forget it," smiled Aftab.

"Round as a marble, deep as a cup, 24 elephants can't lift it up."

Both Pankhuri and Shawn shouted "Well".

"Okay Shawn your chance. Ask something old from your parent's time."

Shawn was all too ready.

"House full, kitchen full, cannot catch a teaspoon full ".

Smoke or Air, Aftab shouted.

29

How To Conceal – Learn From Mrs Sheila Singh

Shawn and Pankhuri were counting the number of days when their parents would meet and thrash out a date, like a farmer thrashing his wheat, for their blissful marriage when all eyes would be ready to receive them as bride and groom and all tongues, even the wagging ones which inevitably caused a wild fire, would be singing praise for the two.

Marriage is so illogical that mathematics fails where one plus one is two but in marriage two become one. Maybe, this is the magic spell and hallucination in which husband and wife pass their full life. The mirage shows the oasis in this desert of love and the two keep running after it without end. Marriage is like the Sahara desert of Africa, almost never ending. The Thar desert of 'Mahro Rajasthan ' in India eclipses the fact from fiction for the two lovers who fail to see right from wrong and continue the unabated love till it's too late and then the knot gets knottier. (naughtier, use the one that best fits you)

Children come and take the sting out of marriage. Such a small baby but occupies the biggest space in our lives and on the bed. The mother and father are crouched and huddled in one corner of the bed while the child rolls all over. He is the centre of attraction where his needs are to be met that instant. Everytime I see a child it reminds me 'everything else in this world can wait, but not so a child '. His wail of tears, brings feet of the parents, not on the trot but on the gallop. He/ She gives such a whale of a time when sick and one smile of his/her brings paradise scurring at your feet.

Shawn at his architectural work-place on his mobile – "Were you, Pankhuri drifting into babie's nappies?"

Pankhuri – "How do you know from so far? Are you a mind reader also?"

Shawn – "So your thoughts and mine are same. I was even thinking of better things but you will push my hands away."

Pankhuri – "Someone will hear, keep quiet. I'm putting my phone down. My love till eternity," in a whisper.

There wasn't even a click sound but the mobile went dead, maybe it (mobile) also understood, -walls have ears. As a child I kept searching for those 'ears' on every wall and even today after so many years I'm still searching. My own ears have been pulled to elephant's ears by my teachers but the ears on the wall remain elusive as ever as the mountain snowman.

Holidays, like buds bursting into flowers, were on the door-step waiting for everyone to pack their bags and be on the serpentine roads of the hills or you want to foray into your happy-go-lucky aunty's house, then take the train.

Shawn's mom on the phone – "Shawn don't you get any leave from your work? I hear, since you joined, you have been working like a dog. A little respite from work will be good for you."

Shawn – "But mom if I take leave, you and dad are going to Assam to fix the marriage date, then what will I do alone at home?"

Mother –"Son, there is a spurt in burglaries here and Sonkar's family, our neighbour, is also going out and there is no one else to look after the house and the dog in our absence.

Shawn- "Mom, I'll come and then you are going with me".

Mom- "Thank you, my pet."

The mobile is such a wonderful invention of the century that it unites any far off outsider. People from India to Australia, to U.S.A, to Honolulu and leaves the people closest, like wife and husband, far off. They are close and yet far away, for the wife is busy connecting people she just knows by name and has no time for him. How can you have time when she is busy from early morning to very late in the night and unfortunately for the poor husband, a day and night has just 24 hours.

Two days later Shawn arrived-his holidays had begun.

Shawn's dad- "What a lovely surprise to see you my son, "as father and son hugged each other."

Shawn's mom – " Hey, won't I get a chance to hold my son?"

Dad- Mr Singh – " Why not? He's my son as much as he is yours. Your mother is getting jealous that he is showering all his love on me and there won't be any left for her. Go cling to her till she gets suffocated and howls for breath. Ha,ha, now tell me how was that?" as she gasped for breath in Shawn's tight grip and kisses that came by the baker's dozens all over her pretty face.

Mom – "My shawn must be hungry as a wolf, as always, (You mean other animals don't feel so hungry) so lets sit at the dining table while I make crispy hot paranthas with omelette and cheese – a favourite of Shawn's."

The smell of pure ghee paranthas permeated the air and the nostrils dilated to soak in the lovely smell and everyone's appetite soared to dig into the hapless (unfortunate) paranthas and carve designs like in childhood but with the hunger look of an abattoir ready with his knife.

Shawn's mum – "Darling, I feel Shawn will be very lonely in the house without us both. Why don't you go alone to Assam or I go. Since the date of marriage is almost fixed and both the parties have only to confirm it, I feel I will do a better job as ladies normally do in such things. At such an hour, I don't wish to leave Shawn alone.

Shawn – "Mum, don't worry about me, I'll be fine."

Mr Singh – " Will you be okay, travelling alone?"

Mrs. Sheila Singh (Shawn's mum) –"Now, I'm not a sixteen year old girl to worry. I'm now an old hag and then the 3-tier sleeper you have booked will be very safe for my plan."

Mr Singh – "Plan, what plan?"

Mrs Sheila Singh- "The plan of you both staying and my going, what else?"

Mr Singh – "I thought you made some plan that I'm not aware of.Okay then, but be careful. I'll put Shawn on the test of 'Walkers and Gazer's company. "

Shawn –"Now, what the hell is this?"

Shawn's mom – "Son, you have finished gazing (looking) at girls and that's how you selected Pankhuri, my sweet-heart. Once you get married, children will come and with them you have to work all day and walk all night to put them to sleep."

Till late you could hear their giggles and laughter.

30

Why Shawn's Mom Had To Travel Alone.

The train was willing to leave Shawn's mother right into Pankhuri's house but was sleepy for she was running over sleepers. And yawning, I heard is contagious. Forty winks is all that is needed for the return journey.

Pankhuri's parents received her with lots of courtesy and love, but were apparently shocked to see two lady's shoes with the lady wearing them and no pair of trousers with a gentleman in it, coming along.

Mrs Singh- (Shawn's mom) – "Aren't you happy to see me, Pankhuri?"

Pankhuri- "We sure are, but a little baffled to see you alone, aunty? Wasn't uncle also coming along?"

Shawn's mom – "Mom and dad, my dear. No more uncle and aunty. "

Pankhuri – "Okay, okay aunty - I mean mom," amidst a burst of laughter from all.

All entwined their necks with Shawn's mom like giraffes and with a peck on each cheek with their pouting lips, all settled down on the sofas which growled when the springs were stretched with tension. Humans, when they are tensed or stressed go to the doctors who prescribes some drugs for relief but where will a poor sofa go except squeak and bear up today with all the weight lifting, it did.

Happiness of marriage had settled down on this house. Only those who have had this privilege will understand how happiness and joy reigns in that house. There is not a single furrow on any forehead for anyone to apply the magical cream of bliss. Everyone is holding the reins of smiles where happiness rains incessantly (without stopping) in the reign of king Shawn and queen Pankhuri. All this at the slightest provocation, turns the house into a medley of mind boggling laughter which becomes difficult, if not impossible, to stop.

Pankhuri's mother – "I was just wondering if 8th- the fat lady of next to next month would be auspicious."

Pankhuri's dad (Mr. Jhunjhunwala)- "What happened, why so late? Didn't we arrive on the phone at an earlier date?"

Shawn's mum- I think Shawn and Pankhuri will run away if the wedding takes place so late. "

Pankhuri's mother – "It is better to run than for us to waste so much money on just one day. "

Pankhuri – "So mom, you are wasting money on the wedding. I think I'll run away right now."

Pankhuri's dad - "What a lovely idea! But why so much delay?"

This was reason enough for everyone to burst into loud guffaws of laughter.

Shawn's mom – "Okay, enough of giggles and laughter, wasn't 22nd, the preferred date the pandit arrived at?"

Pankhuri's mom- "It was and we adhere to it and confirm it. Is it okay with everyone?"

Mr Jhunjhunwala (Pankhuri's dad) – "It is quite close but what the ladies decide is final and which husband can dare and go against the wife –he has to live in the same water as this croc -----. I mean, sorry --- Amen (so be it).

More sweet-meats were laid on the table and since dad was in his element he asked Pankhuri "Is this sweet-meat made of meat (non-vegetarian) that it is called so?" but there were no takers for the stupid question. Everyone's appetite had risen with happiness with the confirmed news.

Shawn's mother was pushing laddos into Pakhuri's mouth and Pankhuri was putting a rasgulla into the big cavity of the mouth of her father.

For humans, birth and marriages are lovely times – a time when even the very cranky, whose full life is eclipsed in only unhappiness, where a ray of joy has not made a mark, brave a pretence of a smile if only for the shutter-bug, for cameras are toting everywhere like a field –marshal his guns on the battle field.

"Did you enjoy the movie we saw late last night?" Shawn's mother quipped.

Pankhuri's mother – "I really got lost in it, so heart-rending."

Pankhuri's father – (munching his special breakfast) "Did any of you hear the back-ground music of this movie?"

Pankhuri's mother - "What back-ground music? We were so engrossed in the movie and where was the time for the lilting back-ground music that you are talking of and who are the idiots who leave the main music for the back-ground music. Silly indeed!"

Pankhuri's dad - This is such a joyous occasion and to dilute it with anything else would only endanger and entitle me to a pessimist when I'm a thorough optimist. (who looks at the lighter side of life). My idea of bringing in such an ugly and insipid (tasteless) topic is to remind you to enjoy every second of your life without hurting anyone and, if possible to bring a crease of a smile to the needy. Live as though this joy of today will never end but keep the death-knell as a back-ground music, never to be heard. The oft repeated quotation on the cremation bus will remind everyone to be good. 'Death is the wish of some, relief of many and the end of all. '

Sorry for this interlude. Let's switch back to the 'Button' of joy.

Pankhuri's mom -"Gone mad, spoiling such a delightful atmosphere. You are such a happy- go –lucky man. Not once since our marriage you have uttered such words "and in a whisper to him "did some incident in our life trigger this? Okay, put on some loud music and back to our revelry of marriage. "

Shawn's mom- "if Shawn's dad was here he would have shouted himself hoarse with glee on the impending marriage of his beloved son."

Pankhuri – "Aun--, sorry mom, show uncle's photograph to my mom. Last time she was not here to see how handsome he is. Mom if you see him, you'll wonder why he didn't come in your life before my dad. See, see my dad hiding his anger behind his broad smile and hey, check my mother's cheeks turning pink with excitement and not with blushing. Sorry, Shawn's mamma your days with Shawn's dad are numbered; my mother is taking over."

There was so much excitement about the marriage that everything was taken as a joke.

Shawn's mother (Mrs. Singh) – "Beta, (normally son, but here daughter) I forgot to bring the purse which had the photograph of Shawn's dad but anyway, bring the other purse which is kept in your almirah, maybe there is a photo."

Pankhuri ran to her almirah, rumpled up some clothes to dig out the purse and brought it to Mrs Singh who unzipped the big, huge purse.

There was a diamond and platinum set, besides the one she already gave Pankhuri, which she now tried on Pankhuri. "A queen for my Shawn" she presented to the rest, turning Pankhuri's face as though she was a doll. There was a crushing hug of Shawn's mum with Pankhuri shouting "long live my mother-outlaw. "There was a lot of laughter and giggles with the word 'out-law' instead of 'in-law'.

Mrs Singh again dug into her unaccountable huge treasure and brought a tie-pin studded with a huge, glittering diamond. "This is for you" as she struggled to put it on Pankhuri's dad's psychedelic tie.

One by one she took out a red-lipstick - a designer nail cutter made in U.S.A, a wrist watch made in Switzerland, more secure in her bag than on her delicate wrist, without a blemish on her white, soft skin. She pulled out a red rose made of some lasting fibre, a souvenir of her marriage, as old as gold and as precious. What she was hunting for in the bag- the photograph – she did not find. She put her delicate fingers again, even peeped inside her colossal purse but nothing that she wanted was there, so she delicately pulled out two gold bangles with her fragile fingers and presented it to Mrs Jhunjhunwala.

Pankhuri's mother – "You already loaded us enough yesterday with so many gifts.

Mrs Singh - "You are talking, as though you haven't harnessed us as horses with innumerable gifts yesterday.

Pankhuri's mother- "I'm so happy, my Pankhuri is getting such a lovely home with such a loving and understanding mother. It's a treasure of a life-time any girl can get. We'll miss you when you go today."

River Kolohe, a tributary of river Brahmaputra flows through quenching the thirst of the Assamese and making the plants stand upright without wilting. A huge fire is disastrous but in small doses it gives warmth, so also is water which NASA (National Aeronautics Space Agency) of USA is searching for, on the Red Planet, Mars. If everything goes well, as expected, scientists will put men on Mars by 2030, as newspapers say.

Pankhuri – "Dad, what are you thinking? Something weird? I could read some of your expressions as you drive, without murmuring a word."

Pankhuri's dad – "You can make a good face reader."

Pankhuri – "I'm your daughter and some traits of your genes must pass on to me."

Mrs Singh (Shawn's mom) was searching for something in her big purse with a worried look.

Pankhuri's mother who was sitting next to her in the car chatting asked "anything wrong?"

Mrs Singh - "Isn't the railway station in front but I feel my ticket is missing. It was in this purse and I'm so particular, but ------------"

Pankhuri's dad as he stopped the car at the side of the road, half on the tar and half on the lovely green grass, the road was heard groaning to the tyres, in their impeccable speech whose frequencies are not in synch with human ears "I loved your long slippery kiss right from home, but now you desert me for greener pastures, two tyres on me and two on the grass. I may be black but very loving. On the other side of the hedge, as is usual, the grass may be greener, but short lived.

The abyss of carelessness was showing and poor Pankhuri's dad with his pretence of smiling was heard "Don't worry I'll turn back home and since it is a confirmed ticket, we can pay the 25% charge to the ticket collector and get a new ticket issued."

Mrs Singh – "I think the house is quite far. We'll pay the extra charge and get a new ticket."

Pankhuri- "Aunty, sorry mom, you'll have to pay not 'WE' "and laughed loud. Before the scenario took an ugly turn and things went out of hand, she pulled out a piece of paper, waved it in the air in front of Shawn's mom and asked "Is this the ticket you are searching?"

Shawn's mom – "You naughty girl, you had it all along and gave us such an agonizing time."

Pankhuri – " It was fun watching each one of you with different expressions. I have clicked each one of you and you can enjoy the funny faces you made."

Pankhuri's mom – "Where did you find it,Pankhuri?"

Pankhuri – "While Shawn's mom was searching for the photograph, this piece of paper fell out from the Big mouth of the purse. I picked it up quietly, saw it was the return ticket and 'Big mouth' whispered to teach mom a lesson on carelessness."

Kamrup Express was waiting for Mrs.Singh (Shawn's mom), as it did for thousands more and with what patience, mother's patience possibly, on the cold, hard iron lines. See the irony of it, it makes people meet with warmth while it gets a cold shoulder all through the winters and a hot berating tongue in the summers just like a husband gets from his wife.

"Okay, okay while the signal is red with anger let me ask you a silly question with an intelligent answer, "quipped Pankhuri.

"What is the difference between a lady, a car and a donkey?" All looked at each other with impatience for the signal could suddenly turn green with envy in their happiness, so Pankhuri let the answers out of the bag.

A lady - Oh dear!

A car - Too dear!

And a donkey ---------- Mrs Singh could not wait for the answer and asked impatiently "and a donkey?"

Pankhuri, quick on her feet as she was with her tongue,

"You dear!"

Mrs Singh – Don't worry, I'm going to be your mother-in-law and I'll teach you who is a donkey and the bogey shook with their laughter and perhaps, woke up the sleeping green signal. The laughter reverberated and could not be subdued long after the train had left leaving in it's trail an emptiness for people who had left each other and a fulfillment for those who had come together. So this was the only work left for trains, to make people meet and depart.

31

Missing You

Pankhuri to the micro-chip in the mobile – "Can't you ring and let me hear Shawn's voice. Almost three hours you have slept silently. You will get fat and won't fit into any mobile. I'll wring (pull) your ears and before she could shame the chip more, it chipped in with a sweet ring. Sure enough it was Shawn. His voice converted into signals reached the towers where it was deflected into the skies to be beamed back to the Earth right into the ears of Pankhuri where it poured it's sweetness.

Pankhuri – "Sorry, sorry for the harsh words. You are so sweet."

Shawn – "Which harsh words, I didn't hear any?"

Pankhuri – "Cha, cha I was not talking to you. "

Shawn – "Who else is there, then?"

Pankhuri -"There is nobody here, except mum in the other room. "

Shawn – "Then ------?"

Pankhuri – "Nobody, I was talking to the micro-chip in my mobile. "

Shawn –"my Pankhuri is getting mad. Talking to the chip in the mobile, next she will be talking to the walls, which have ears and then the world will know her inner – most secrets."

Pankhuri –"Okay, okay you boys don't care and that is the reason for your aloofness."

Shawn – I think clocks and watches are running on mud wheels and that is why time is passing with difficulty. There is still some days to go and I wonder how I will pass them. Time seems to be dragging with very heavy feet. "

Pankhuri – (Who was feeling dejected tries to lighten Shawn) "Don't be a pessimist, (who sees half the glass of water empty) be the optimist (who sees half the glass of water full) that you are. These few days will be over in a jiffy. " A cloud of happiness descended on both.

A fifty year old man has a claustrophobic apprehension of his wife, then how come he is so stupid at 18 to get no smell of her designs and gets stuck in her web like what the Widow spider does to her male.

Where am I veering off? A disgruntled man can't think of anything better than to spoil somebody's love life. That's how all the people in the world are out to throttle each other.

Shawn – "Wow, that's nice hearing from someone who reminds me everyday how many days to go and how difficult it is for her, as time is passing at snail speed."

Pankhuri – "Dodo (stupid) stop it. Maybe someone is hearing you." Then her eyes moved furtively all around but it was futile for she saw no one around till a sweet, familiar voice rang out from the back. It was her mom. "You didn't look at your back. I was sneaking from there. When a girl comes of age, the mother has to be extra vigilant. So you want to deprive your mother of your secrets with Shawn. I love you my dahling and I want you always happy."

Pankhuri – "You naughty mama, I wish everyone gets a mother like you- Shawn my mama loves you too.

Shawn –(who was still on the mobile) – "Give your mom a bear hug from my side and remind her 'I love her too'. She will love the bear hug when I give it in person and she hears the cracking of her rib-cage."

32

FUNNY DAY DREAMS

The days seem to be dragging as though a space shuttle was entering the Earth's atmosphere and needed the maximum velocity to overcome the friction and gravitational pull, which was not forth-coming.

If Shawn and Pankhuri were not engrossed in talking over the phone, Shawn would take time off from his architectural plans on which he was pouring and dive into the abyss of her memory. He would go into a reverie and only when his co-worker friends would snap their fingers in front of his eyes would he realize the situation he was in.

His brain was swimming with her thoughts. Even in his thoughts, if he tried to gather her in his arms she would slip away like an eel. "Be careful, your neighbours are watching us", she would in her lilting voice sing. He would want to hear that voice again and yet again, so soft and sweet it sounded. In his imagination, hand-in –hand he would visit Honolulu, Disney World of Las Vegas, which is anybody's dream from small to even frail people whose one leg would be dangling in the grave.

"Pankhuri try your hand at this" pointing to a game of minting machine spitting coins like a hose-pipe spurting water in your garden.

With her fragile, delicate fingers she tried her luck and had it been a state lottery she would have amassed a wealth to be in the bracket of a billionaire.

Their feet were not on the ground and their spirits higher – who wouldn't be if your fingers were entwined in love.

"Would you be scared going in that Roller-Coaster? Just see the people upside down at that height and at that speed," inquired Shawn more to hear that she had implicit faith in him.

Pankhuri – "Not when you have your arms around to protect me."

His mind went berserk wool-gathering till he saw Pankhuri sky-diving and the parachute refusing to open. In the melee that followed, he banged himself on the table he was working on, much to the consternation (surprise) of his colleagues and chagrin and embarrassment of his own.

Pankhuri was no better. She also would day-dream besides normally in the night.

Pankhuri – "Shawn, what happened to your teeth?"

Shawn – "I'm a Dracula and I have come to suck your blood. Yipee, yew ------"

Pankhuri would jump up with a shriek or she would see Shawn being carried away by the white tiger in Delhi zoo as it happened in real life when the auto-driver trying to click photographs from close, slipped and fell a prey to the tiger. It was heart-rending to watch the video on the mobile which went viral. Almost for a minute the man with folded hands begged the tiger to spare his life. The tiger sat in front as though enjoying the scene as much as GOD ALMIGHTY enjoys the scare of the poor with folded hands beseeching HIM to let them live for a few days more. If wishes were horses, beggars would ride. The ULTIMATE POWER refuses to hear the cry of the poor as much as the tiger did and carried the poor driver away as though it was a toy and a play-thing. Pankhuri would pray such thoughts do not enter her brain but they were adamant like alcohol which refuses to leave the drunkards and refuses to listen to their (drunkards) entreaties. Such thoughts made a regular feature of her thoughts and she felt herself helpless in thwarting such ominous, lecherous occasions.

Pankhuri – "Shawn, Shawn I saw the white tiger of Delhi zoo who carried the poor rickshawala carry you too in broad daylight. Is it a premonition (sign) to anything bad coming?"

Shawn – "Why do you even think of such things? Nothing bad can ever come our way when Providence has brought us together and we are like two Siamese twins- never to be separated "and to make light of it and alienate her from such thoughts he told her this sickening joke he read on the mobile his friends had sent him.

One friend to another- "When you are around 70 years old, your life-span is over. Now which disease would you like to have. You have to choose one. The list is (1) Heart disease (2) Kidney Failure (3) Parkinson Disease and (4) Alzheimer Disease.

Pankhuri would reply very innocently forgetting her dreams.

Heart disease I cannot get. I have already given you my heart.

With all the beer we had in college together, my kidneys are totally flushed and they are kid-knees (Kidneys)- too young to get any disease.

Parkinson's disease (hands shaking involuntarily) I feel you should get. You love shaking hands with each and everyone. Ha, ha.

Alzheimer's disease (forgetting, here she means forgetting her husband) I don't mind in old age. Telling her husband Shawn- "Who are you old, fat pig lying on my bed?"

33

BITTER SWEET TALK OF THE WIVES.

It is usually very cumbersome to invite people for a wedding. Whose name will be on the list of invites is not an easy matter for even acquaintances want their names on the list.

Shawn in his office – "Mr Shyam Lal you are so handsome but today, why is your face so long, like a horse?"

Mr Shyam Lal – "Gurmeet invited you for his party, Shawn but conveniently forgot me. Then what do you expect, if not a long horse's face? Just the other day he borrowed Rs 50/- from me since he had no change."

Shawn in a lighter vein for he was in a mood to laugh – "Shyam, don't you know the difference between a friend and an acquaintance? An acquaintance is a friend you know well enough to borrow from but not well enough to lend to".

Mr Shyam Lal- "Stop it Shawn and don't you dare forget me for your wedding along with my family."

Shawn – "I'm trying with all my might to forget you but it will only go slowly."

Shyam –"Okay, okay. You know Shawn, everyone in this office calls me Mr Nasty. I --------

Shawn cuts him short – "Hey dude, you know your name very well?"

Shyam Lal – "I am a great thinker, philosopher. They say 'Heaven is a place where all wrongs will be made right' then why should I worry".

All eyes turned towards the mellowed Shyam Lal, some even looked cock-eyed especially those lazy ones who did not even flex their neck muscles to turn to see Mr Shyam Lal's change of stance from Mr Nasty to a cheer –leader. The act that Shawn performed on Shyam Lal took everyone's breath away as though it (breath) was lying on the table and Shawn, the thief stole it.

Someone's rusty mouth opened to crack another mobile joke but was choked with a spoil-sport "Let's finish our work then we'll have a session."

Those who had self-imposed punishment of standing were back in the arms of their second wives, yes the office chairs where they spent five days of the week. Those who were getting cock-eyed were happy to get relief from the strain of their eyes and happier were the chairs to get all the concentration of their estranged bed-fellows, sorry sitting-fellows.

Now all this conglomeration of architects sat down with the sole aim of providing beautiful, comfortable houses for the thousands of handsome dudes and their bevy of beauties to transform them to husband and wife with the warmth that only flows from a home and never a house.

These were some of the tactics Shawn employed which were up his sleeves to pass the time. I have seen and heard only magicians have tricks up their sleeves, so Shawn was a magician on the quiet and an architect in the open.

The day of the wedding was slowly but surely creeping surreptiously on the two, Pankhuri and Shawn, who were waiting anxiously for the two little ducklings (number 22) of 'Housie fame', the allotted, selected day by the purohit for the wedding. Even the invited guests, especially the ladies were busy preparing the designer blouses for their silk embroidered sari.

"Darling just zip my blouse from the back? Will this pearl necklace go with it or should I wear that tantalizing diamond one? This shoe is not looking so nice, it's just not matching. I think, dahling, I'll go and buy a golden shoe. Won't I look smashing, dahling? I think many of the ladies will burn holes in their sarees (our Indian dress) out of jealousy, seeing me look so gorgeous."

Husband –" I'm feeling so scared that this boy, What's his name? The one getting married, yes, yes, Shawn may leave that girl and go after the smashing beauty, you."

Wife – "You know I don't like such silly jokes and don't cut me spoiling the flow of what I was saying. Now where was I? Oh yes, remember that dark, flat faced lady dressed so gaudily, looking every inch a butter-fly, my foot, a moth trying to draw everyone's attention as though she was 'the Leaning Tower of Pisa '. The only trump card she had was 'my husband is the D.M. (District Magistrate) of this burgeoning city.' Dahling are you so dumb that you could not even get through the I.A.S. (Indian Administrative Service) to become the D.M, I wish I knew you were good for nothing. I wouldn't have married you."

Don't you think, women should have no fetters and should be free like the girls of the west? Here we get married to one, stick to one even if he is good-for- nothing? 'Mama se pooch darling', (ask my mother) rear his children, be in the kitchen, sweep, swab and then her (Husband) comes home asking audaciously what have you done the whole day? Come, press my back, a little. Arre, arre, don't you have any strength to press? Just see your thick manly hands and see your unkempt hair? I wish I could throttle his neck for him. "

If I carry on showing such scenes depicting your own daily life volumes and volumes of this book will be needed with the end still receding in the distance with no exit for the bitter-sweet talk.

She'll besmirch you brusquely in one tone and the next would be honey-drops dipped in chocolate for the easy-peasy (easy) going husband who grins inanely (silly) for all this caper (activity). He is so clever not to retaliate or be a kill-joy (spoil sport) or what a fiasco poor fellow has to face.

Pankhuri- "Is everything okay, Shawn? I'm so jittery and worried and getting a premonition that something amiss will happen."

Shawn – "People usually make a mountain of a mole-hill. You make out of nothing. Please keep your nerves in place and be cool. Nothing is going to happen and I'm with you."

Pankhuri- "You never told me how you are coming? Which day and what time? Just three days are left and I have got butterflies in my stomach."

Shawn in a jocund mood – "fly the butterflies in the mean-time and count their myriad colours, Ha, ha. Day-after at 3 pm we fly and reach after 2 hours 10 minutes. Mum is so excited she is taking even our neighbour three houses away whose handsome son with curly hair in our college had a keen eye on you, remember."

Pankhuri – "I cannot remember anyone except you."

Shawn tantalizing her more- "The one who even brought his mother to the college to make friends with you and sent you the butter coloured yellow roses which you turned down. His handsome face struck you now, I'm sure?"

Pankhuri – "Enough Shawn."

Shawn- "Okay, okay, we are six people coming and I have already messaged all the particulars to your dad."

Pankhuri – "Are you pulling my legs? Only six baratis (guests). Won't people laugh?"

Shawn – "Yes, yes, people are sitting just to count the number of baratis. Should I go with the invitation cards on the road-side and ask strangers to answer some silly questions like 1) What is your name? 2) Do you have a handkerchief in your pocket? and 3) Do you have a Re1 coin in your pocket? and those who answer the last two questions with a 'Yes' have won the jack-pot and are invited for our wedding."

Pankhuri - "Shawn you are good in entertaining people and I love you for your weird ideas. Clasp me tight, when we are married, so that I don't hear your nonsense. Ha, ha, love you baby. I think mum is yelling her lungs out for me. Bye handsome "

Shawn – "What do you want?"

Pankhuri – "I don't understand?"

Shawn – "You only said handsome."

Pankhuri – "Leave your silly jokes alone. Love you and bye." She hung up.

With all his jokes and with an easy –going life-style, Shawn was very uneasy himself passing that day. Shawn thinking, but perhaps his tongue couldn't keep secrets, it blurted to himself – "So easy to lecture someone but so difficult to implement it, yourself. "He had a sneer on his face and was laughing at himself. "Don't know what the other boys do when just two days eclipses them from going to the bride's house." As though on request, uninvited voices like uninvited guests in a wedding filled him. One said "Enjoy every moment of your freedom till the knot of marriage ties you". Another rang out "Hold her close in your fantasy "and yet another boomed "be your normal self and relax."

In this context of 'could he' or 'could he not' the wipers of his eyes, the eye-lids were switched off like the wipers on a car and he was in the Disneyland of his dreams, holding Pankhuri to his heart's content and she cooing like a dove in his strong-hold.

Morning came with the glimpse of rays trying to shatter his sleep but his father, as usual, alert about his son's comfort, drew the curtains to keep the sunlight away so that he rested enough. Shawn's mother even came to wake him for break-fast but the father pulled her away with a whisper "let him rest fully".

It was almost afternoon when one needle of the clock gets lost. Yes, it was exactly 12 O'clock.

34

To The Airport

How two days had passed for the two taxi fellows were honking to take the two families to the air-port.

The neighbour's family all excited with bag and baggage were sitting in the drawing room sipping tea. Rasogullas, rasmalai and the famous motichoor ka laddu (all Indian sweets) adorned the table tempting the neighbours to stretch their hands to pick one. "No thank you" when offered, when inside was aflame with 'just you go in the other room and then you see what all vanishes from the delectable sweets into our stomachs. This trait of humans is very notice-able in parties and weddings where the hosts are busy elsewhere. The plates are so full that a normal person cannot eat and the cause of a lot of wastage. The grand-mother is scolding "why do you eat so much in a party that you vomit as you come home. There is a big queue for the toilets as loose motions have let loose their reign of terror.

They are asking for the flight tickets," echoed Shawn's father to the mother who was incharge of the tickets, as usually she was. Check-in of the luggage was done and frisking time (since they were not V.I.P) a stray pin on the blouse of Shawn's mother alerted the buzzer till the culprit was traced from it's hiding place. All had a hearty laugh but I give credence to the security for being so vigilant in doing their duty – but for them, we would have so many mishaps. I take my hat off in gratitude. I wish everyone in India did their duty with honesty and we can sing with pride 'East or West, my India is the best.'

Trilok Ladla, as the curly haired boy was called, sat between Shawn's father and Shawn. The two mothers and Mr Ladla sat in the front row. The planes engine whirred but did not take to the skies. It seems there was a wait for some V.I.P.(very important person) and the plane was side-lined where it halted for more than two hours before that puny, funny looking man arrived with a lot of fanfare. The staff on duty stood in a row welcoming him while all the passenger' s blood was on the boil- very many were getting late for some meetings as was shawn and his family for a different but very important reason. All this time, the two ladies skipped from one topic to another related mostly to gold, sarees and their favourite topic of gossiping about other ladies, who they laid thread-bare and after every one incident of gossip there would be a loud giggle, a signal for the next victim or second episode.

Mrs Ladla to Shawn- "Son, I can't reach the suitcase, it is too high?"

Mr Ladla before Shawn could get up- "Darling, why don't you try with your long tongue. "

There was such a loud thud of laughter that even people who were not supposed to join in the fun were very much in it and Mrs Ladla response was shrouded in it.

Trilok Ladla- "You are so lucky Shawn, to get such a nice, cultured girl like Pankhuri and she is so lucky to have a jewel like you."

Shawn – "Yaar, (friend) I heard you sent yellow roses for Pankhuri, when I had not come in her life and she had returned it with thanks."

Trilok Ladla – "She told you about this incident, did she?"

Shawn – "Ya, and many more proposals that she had. You know where there is honey, flies are bound to come."

Trilok Ladla –"You know the best man wins and I have come with you willingly to see that she is happy. I'll be happy in her happiness."

Shawn – "I have yet to see a guy like you, so considerate, so thoughtful and if had met you earlier I would have paved the way towards Pankhuri, for you."

Trilok Ladla – "Don't even harness such thoughts, I will feel ashamed. Right now my slate is clean and when miss Right comes she will not miss being my misses (Mrs)."

Shawn – "She must be waiting in some nook or corner for you – I'm sure, she will be lovely to behold."

At the very start, Shawn's dad had feigned that he had slept, when his ears were flapping like that of a bat's antennae. He realized that his son had a heart of gold and even Trilok Ladla was a real gentleman, who any girl should be proud to have as a husband.

Unlike most pilots, the aeroplane had a soft landing without a thud. As stipulated, the time it took to reach was exactly 2 hours 10 minutes unlike the unpredictable trains which can reach their destination as and when it likes with no one responsible for the delay. This was the first time, the two boys took time off to look at the pretty, smart air-hostesses.

To lead them out of the plane was Mrs Ladla along with her son, Trilok, holding her hand and guiding her out of the exit followed by Shawn's mom and dad and the last was Shawn himself, trying to see nothing was left behind in the plane. The air-hostesses and the stewards were courteous as ever and so was the co-pilot. There was no sign of the pilot, either he was busy with the instruments on his panel or some crazy air-hostess. The way was all carpeted in turquoise blue and looked more of a tunnel. All heaved a sigh of relief for the comfortable journey and stretched themselves with smiles on their faces. In that instant, Shawn's mom missed a step and went bang into Mr and Mrs Ladla who went flying down. Fortunately it was just a fall of three steps but for the on-lookers it was a comical sight. Not so for the Singh family for Shawn's dad tried to catch hold of his wife who somehow he could stop but went head-long down himself, sprawling on the clean cemented portion. Even if he tried licking the dust, there was nothing for him to feed on, so clean was the place. Shawn had lunged forward to hold his parents but had failed for a split-second delay. Now he stood holding the railing and laughing at the scene just three steps away, but when he saw Trilok trying to pick his dad and failing he felt his dad was hurt. In one leap he hurtled himself down and was beside his father trying to ease him up. Futility reigned and the staff on duty sent for a doctor. He was put on a stretcher and with Shawn to accompany him was taken by the doctor somewhere closeby. The rest ie. Mr and Mrs Ladla, Trilok and Shawn's mom went with Pankhuri's crowd who had come to receive them after they had collected the luggage from the rotating belt.

Shawn's dad was not badly hurt but it would take 2-3 days for him to walk. Nice time for a father to relax, when the son should be sitting taking the pheras.

35

Getting Ready

Shawn was uneasy and did not have even the proverbial forty winks in the night. Morning dawned and his eyes automatically closed. All had breakfast but nobody disturbed him. As heavy as lead, that's what his eye-lids weighed. The eye-lashes did quiver to open but the ciliary muscles were not strong like an ox to pull quintals and quintals of flour from the Flour-mill to the wholesale and retail dealers. He slept on and on oblivious of the world outside but on the screen of his closed eyes, the oldest invention of man-kind – the closed-circuit T.V of his eyes- in which he and Pankhuri played the lead roles, reclining on each other and completely inebriated in each other's love with no villain to spoil the show. Now it dawned on him that real life-size realities also exist and in his case, like the dream, there were no villains. He opened his eyes, rubbed them clear of the dreams and saw two loving eyes peering into him showering petals of concern and love that no one except a mother can do and indeed she was the doting mother. He gathered her in his arms and planted so many kisses on them that if you visit the place today, a huge Kissing tree is in full bloom.

Shawn 's roving eyes searched for his father-" Did anyone go to see dad? I want to go and see him right now."

Mrs Sheila Singh (Shawn's mother) – "Trilok, Mr Ladla and Pankhuri 's father, Mr Jhunjhunwala all went to see him in the hospital and found him in high spirits inquiring about his son. I'll go with you and even Mrs. Jhunjhunwala wants to come along with us. Aren't you hungary my son?"

Shawn – "No mama, I'm in Honolulu and not Hungary."

Shawn's mother – "A slip of the tongue is no fault of mine but those who remind are most unkind. I meant hungry and not Hungary- the country, North-East of Austria.

Shawn- "Clap for mama, we all know she was good in History; today we know she is good in geography too but I feel dad wouldn't marry her if her geography was not good."

Shawn's mum- " Don't be naughty?"

Shawn – "Okay, okay my sweetie mama, I was just pulling your leg,"as he pulled her tighter in his arms till she shrieked. "So you were trying to impress me with this old quotation that you picked up from some grave."

Shawn's mom-"Your maternal grand-mother used it on us many times and I used it on you today."

Shawn – "Borrowed words, like borrowed garments never fit well but you used it so appropriately and at the right moment and time when the iron was hot. I bow my head to thee. You are as wise as an owl or is it King Solomon, but isn't this night bird, the owl, ominous. In Indian literature, the owl is considered foolish. Let's get started, aren't we already running late."

Shawn had used the razor-sharp blade yesterday and he purposely used it today. He normally cut himself with a brand new blade and he didn't want any cuts and bruises on his wedding day, like a wounded soldier. He used the after-shave; his face smarted slightly but the tinge of pain turned to freshness. He wore his usual clothes. His mother was still grappling with the jewelry for she didn't want to change it again when she dressed for the wedding. Lunch was befitting a bride-groom. Pankhuri's dad had taken special care to see the best of everything was in place for them. There was no demand of a dowry which was very unusual in a wedding in India. It was more like no camels in the world's largest Sahara desert in Africa or in our own Thar desert in Rajasthan. The Ladla family was also sitting with them for lunch. The two mothers were in constant touch via the mobiles and were treated more like family members than neighbours. Even Trilok and Shawn were sharing Jokes and had a good rapport with each other. The other two men were already quite familiar with each other and even with each other's wives when they were in Pankhuri's house.

Shawn was ready to go and see his father along with his mother and Trilok. Shawn was supposed to pick up Pankhuri's mother from their house and felt he may get a glimpse of Pankhuri but Mrs Ladla, who was a little conservative asked if it was right for Shawn to meet Pankhuri before the wedding. It was considered a bad omen in some cultures. "What different rituals they have?" thought Shawn, without airing his views. The idea just receeded in the distance and he bore the reluctance calmly.

Mrs Ladla to wipe all traces of it – "Patience is the mother of virtue and you are such an obedient son. We are sure you won't harp on it again.

Shawn's Mom- "Besides Pankhuri and her Mom are at the beauty parlour and you know it takes a lot of time. It is possible they may come straight from there to the wedding venue."

Shawn –"We do not know the way to the pandal? How will we reach there?"

Mrs Singh – "Arre beta, Mr Jhunjhunwala will come to fetch us and don't worry about anything. We are here."

They reached the hospital where Mr Singh was singing to recuperate.

Mr Singh- "Shawn, just draw the curtain?"

Shawn –"Sorry dad, I have no pencil and no paper." That was enough to break the ice and then there was laughter and more laughter and the oppressed atmosphere was filled with an invigorating, freshly filtered oxygen to wipe out the dampened air.

Trilok – "Uncle, a traffic police catches a man for rash-driving and asks for the driving licence."

The man with humour- "I ain't have any. I'm still a trainee and learning driving. "

Policeman – "Then where is your trainer?"

Man innocently-"Sir, I'm doing correspondence course."

There was such a huge laughter that even Mr Singh nearly jumped from his bed, forgetting that the doctor forbade his movement.

Shawn was very happy that his father was in high spirits and with the comforting words that his loving dad uttered "I'm with you always even if I am lying on this bed. Soon I'll be with you. Enjoy every moment of your marriage."

Shawn's Mom- "Now the time is almost 4 O'clock, I feel we all should start getting ready. We could easily be late and I hate to keep people waiting. Shawn get into your sherwani."

Mr Ladla- "I feel we should go to our room and get ready for the wedding. "

Mr Ladla shaving and feeling the smoothness with his hand to his wife –"See mama, aren't my cheeks as smooth as the ice of Canada? Try skiing on it. "

Mrs Ladla – "We have no time for your crap. We also have to dress."

Mr Ladla – If such sharp razor blades were available earlier, very few people would have had to hide their handsome faces behind a beard. It may have the best razor sharp edge but even today they are no match for my wife's tongue.

Trilok – "Then dad, why do you go spending so much money on blades, when such a sharp one sleeps with you every night."

Trilok's mother – "Trilok, Trilok you are also getting wings like your father."

Mr Ladla – "Son, you know I write for the Sunday magazine. Today, I have unearthed two truths about my writing, Trilok, my son, one day you will also get married and that is reason enough for you to know. Everytime I opened my mouth to speak my wife told me to shut up, so I took to writing. Hear more ahead – I'm so hen –pecked that my writing has turned to fowl-scratches. Trilok why didn't you join in the laugh?"

Trilok - "Dad it is better for you to fall apart alone then for me to join you (With gum), and then I don't want to fire mum's ire (anger) on me.I still have a long way to get married and I don't want mum to put the chastity belt on my wife and throw the keys away. The father –son duo joins in and the mother leaves for dressing to the other room with a huff.

Trilok – "Dad, why do people ask only for the girl's hand in marriage?"

Mr Ladla – "Because the rest of the body comes free – buy one, get one free. "(Giggles)

36

Shawn In A Sherwani

Shawn in a gold brocade sherwani with a sehra of a garland of marigold blocking most of his view with slight chinks in the armour of a bride-groom, waiting in a beautiful pandal (shamiana), decorated for the occasion for his bride –to-be, Pankhuri. His mother stood at his side consoling him that Pankhuri could arrive any minute, dressed as a queen with four ladies-in-waiting holding veils of flowers on four light poles. The band would strike a lovely note of music as the bride walked slowly towards the groom which was her destined destination for eternity in the seven lives she would be bestowed with. Trilok with a pink sehra of cloth stood behind Shawn like a real friend hearing and witnessing all the scenes enthusiastically which he would relate to Shawn in whispers, loud enough for even Shawn's mother to hear. Shawn's own view was curtailed due to the din of the music playing. Mr Jhunjhunwala along with Mr Ladla were at the gate warmly welcoming guests and reminding them not to go without partaking a little morsel of food spread out in the banquet hall's building. They were all wearing pink sehras on their head for easy recognition and that they were very close knit.

"Doctor, please welcome " as Pankhuri's dad introduced him to Mr Ladla. "He's an excellent physician, Dr Mittal and here's his sweet wife."

"Meet the eminent Principal of SF school, Mr Merchant and his bubbly wife, Sangeeta as she pressed an envelope into his hand, a present for the couple. Pankhuri's dad passed the envelope into a very trusted hand who carried a huge bag containing all these gifts. Later, every name would be entered with the specific amount. This is almost identical to the 'Wishing Well' where all the presents are left for the couple in the other community. In the western countries, they even send you to a particular shop to buy the gifts, so that no two gifts are the same. Others send you an envelope with 'Your presence and your present will be much appreciated '.Different ways to make the couple stand firmly on their feet.

"Hullo, welcome, welcome he is Mr Gupta, the chief engineer of PWD and he is Mr Ladla, a very close friend."

"Meet a very warm friend, always helping anyone, the man with the best ironed, biggest and matching turban in full Guwahati, Mr Gurbachan Singh.

Mr Gurbachan Singh- "I loved the shenai playing from the machan in front of the beautifully decorated gate, heralding the marriage. From here the place inside looks like

Disneyland has come to stay. I'll go and see for myself further."

Mr Ladla – "Very talkative and looks every inch a thorough gentleman from the little that is audible from the din of the noise."

Here comes the children's favourite aunty, Dr Meera-loved by one and all.

The queue of well-wishers was growing.

Shawn's mum – Shawn there is a custom of hiding the groom's shoes and all you have to do is please and placate the girls with the demand of money. Your shoes will then find their rightful owner – your feet. There will also be the ceremony of Kanyadaan, putting the Sindoor and of course, what you are waiting for, the seven pheras with Pankhuri around the Agni-kund while the pundits will be busy reciting Shloks which have a lot of meaning, but who has the time to hear? All want to get married and go for their honey-moon. By the way, your dad has booked two plane tickets for your honey-moon to Simla."

Shawn – "I have the best mum and dad in the world "as he squeezed his mother's hand.

The kaleidoscope of different types of people pouring in was clearly visible by the euphoria of ecstasy on their cheerful faces. The medley of people in their best attire, some in blue suits, some in black, some in gorgeous pink, white, turquoise blue and red sarees looked as though the whole city had turned up for a fancy dress masquerading only as a king, queen, prince and princess with their impeccable clothes.

The delectable food showed it's presence with the aroma it splattered all around exactly the way a scent bottle does. The nostrils just absorbed the Flavor and the feet turned it's direction trudging towards the food court. Those who wanted to build an appetite rushed to the dais where the bride-groom sat waiting for his bride. Everywhere photographers clicked with their flashes on and at times it looked like lightening struck the place with so many cameras at one time.

Everybody tried their hand at guessing.

One guest – "I think the bride is still dressing?"

Another – "I feel she is still stuck at the beauty parlour."

And yet another – "I think they want the bride to rest but the poor bride-groom must be tired waiting."

A beaming lady – "Oh, ho; that's why the men keep their women –folk waiting at home while they are out, enjoying."

37

THE BRIDE'S ARRIVAL

Pankhuri's mother arrived from somewhere inside where she was busy as a bee and now stretched her legs sitting next to Shawn's mother and inquiring what she had sent from inside, did they get to eat?"

MRs Singh – "Oh, you did all that and here we were on pins and needles to know where you are. Come, I'll help you."

Mrs Jhunjhunwala – "You are doing wonderfully well by meeting the people. Oh gosh; here comes the bride. Doesn't she look pretty? A queen fit for Shawn, the king. She took one step at a time, very daintily, lady-like as though others take two steps at a time. You people please don't smile, unnecessarily your face muscles will be stretched in exercise.

Pankhuri's full smiling face was open whereas Shawn's manly, handsome face was totally covered with the sehra. Later the ladies languish in a 'Ghunghat' (veil) and the male species go scot-free.

The bride tip-toed on the three steps as though she was on a precipice, but the maids- in- waiting stood by her. She took another step where Shawn opened his palms and she slid her nimble, delicate, fragile fingers into it. As she sat down, tears of happiness welled up in Mrs. Jhunjhunwala's eyes, as she and Shawn's mother kissed her.

"Wipe those moist eyes, Trilok," Mrs Ladla whispered in his ears. "All will wonder, why, if they notice?"

Trilok smiling –"I have no duster to wipe this black-board. " (face)

Two garlands appeared from somewhere for the 'Jaimala' ceremony.

Pankhuri was lifted high up in the air by her friends and poor Trilok alone could not lift Shawn high enough to garland Pankhuri. There was much booing but Shawn being an optimist didn't mind stooping to conquer or as he had learnt in school 'win as though you are used to it and lose as though you enjoyed it for a change' and here was a situation where you won both ways.

Trilok just whispered in Shawn's ears that he would be back soon and without waiting for a reply vanished.

Shawn's mother was herself caught as the guests came to know she was the bride-groom's mother. She enjoyed being beckoned with so much love and yet felt uneasy inside for some reason of her own. Guests were scattered all over, some enjoying the delicacies served time and again to them; others just enjoying the scene where the purohit (Priest) was chanting mantras.

The fire in the Agni-kund (fire-place) was roaring red in the face belching only heat being fed by the pandit with pure ghee. Lovely shloks paved the way into many hearts who preferred to listen. Anyone will go gaga over the meanings if he is unbiased, but then all the holy books teach you good things. 'Mala pheri din gaya, gaya na man ka pher '(We keep turning the beads of the rosary till the day goes, but what is inside our head – the dirt stays). We remember everything but fail to be good which is their basic aim. We are so prejudiced and biased with no patience for other faiths. There is one God and we are all one big family. In times of happiness we are Indians, Pakistanis, Dutch, Americans, Australians, Russians and Europeans etc ready to fight with each other. Let a calamity come like the seas and oceans drowning even mount Everest (29,028 feet above sea –level) then all the nations of the world be it atheists, Christianity, Hinduism, Islam, Zoroastrians will all unite to save themselves and mankind. Think, that's all I ask of you?

As man grows old, some disease or the other is waiting for him with open arms. Nobody in the world can avoid this for old age is the biggest disease till scientists find a way out. Where are we going and what do we want from life? If happiness is all that we want from life, go ahead and enjoy it to the brim and let others enjoy along. If there is something beyond happiness then my lips are sealed.

38

The Seven Pheras

The first Phera around the Agni Kund, which was blazing was over and Shawn felt peace of mind descending on him from high above. It runs through your body with a slight shiver traversing from top to the legs and that's what had happened to the maelstrom of different emotions that he felt maimed earlier with and now settled.

"How pretty she looks with such an angelic face," commented one of the guests.

"The boy is equally handsome, what a lovely couple they make, "whispered another loud enough to be audible.

If eyes could absorb beauty, then today there was a crowd pulsating in that wave with guffaws of laughter and happiness.

39

EYES OPENED

The fifth Phera was culminating to it's logical end of eternal happiness, when a silhouette of two people, one on a wheel-chair and the other walking slowly towards the Agni Kund was seen at a distance.

Man proposes, God disposes. Amidst the atmosphere of this din of joy and laughter one spark big enough flew from the warmth of the Agni Kund to the knot of the couple. Before anybody could rise to the occasion, the knot had burnt to ashes and cinder without touching Pankhuri and Shawn. Everybody jumped up with screams of cries but one shriek, loud and shrill rose to such a crescendo that all eyes turned towards it. It was Pankhuri's mother, who else but a mother could have emanated such a whale of a wail of a shriek and tears, maiming and drowning every other sound with it.

For the first time, Shawn's dad sitting in the wheel-chair, pushed by Trilok who had gone to fetch him from the hospital to witness his son's pheras, faced the mother and daughter and froze as though a cobra hissed in front of his eyes ready to strike and paralyse him. In that split second Pankhuri's mother lifted her gazelle eyes filled with tears, saw Shawn's dad and turned into a statue and then swooned into a heap of pulp as though all bones in her body had melted. When a human being passes all stages of stress and tribulations and cannot bear more, nature has secured a weapon to fight it – fainting.

Gosh! In such a cordial and fun-filled atmosphere, how did the icy tentacles of this ruthless and lecherous sadness gouge everyone's vision to show it's presence. Everyone was thunder-struck. What had happened then? A marriage of bliss had maneuvered itself to blisters. It was not even a case of marry in a hurry and repent at leisure.

40

What You Sow, Will One Day Re-Appear.

Surely the adage 'there is many a slip between the cup and the lip 'stood firmly in it's saddle since some enterprising writer penned it. How I wish I could thank him for quoting it. How a lovely wedding had turned to ashes.

If you turn to logic there is no smoke without fire.

Did the history of the two statues (Mrs Jhunjhunwala – Pankhuri's mother and Mr Singh (Shawn's dad) have anything to do with such a catastrophe?

Till they found their frozen tongues thawed no answers would be forth-coming. Patience was what all had to take refuge with.

While all were waiting, someone was scurrying away taking refuge, away from this marriage pandal, but all were so shocked and in their shells to observe. Shawn's dad, Mr Singh was the first to shake himself from this gruesome death of doomsday.

Leave alone humans, even clouds weep in the form of rains and thunder when depression in the air sets in a particular place.

Mr Jhunjhunwala (Pankhuri's father) – "Why all this commotion Mr Singh?"

Mr Singh (Shawn's dad) – shaking himself from his stupor to compose himself- "A brother and sister cannot get married. It would amount to incest."

It was such a blow that it hammered everyone's brains out of their skull.

Mr Jhunjhunwala (Pankhuri's dad) – "What do you mean by all this? Our brains cannot fathom the depth of all this?"

Mr Singh (Shawn's dad) – "I repeat Shawn and Pankhuri are brother and sister."

Mr Jhunjhunwala (Pankhuri's father)- "How can you say such a thing with so much certainty?"

Mr Singh – "Because Shawn and Pankhuri (earlier Shaan and Petula) are both my children. Let your wife, Mrs Jhunjhunwala regain her composure and everything will be crystal clear. Even you maybe able to throw some light on this? When you got married to your wife, wasn't she a married lady with two children? I was her first husband but she threw me like a dirty handkerchief when she fell in love with you. But not being a cantankerous person (bad tempered), I just let her go without an acrimonious (angry and strong words) divorce. She wanted to keep Petula

(now Pankhuri), the girl and gave me the boy, Shaan, which by clerical error turned to Shawn. I loved her but I wanted her happy, so I let her go. But what coincidence is this, to bring us again together and under such circumstances. God you are great to save us at the last minute from such an ignominious death. Surely, I could have not survived. Thank you, God..

From the deafening silence rose a voice, that of Shawn- "Thank you God for saving us at the last minute. God has been very kind to keep the sacred name of brother and sister intact. I know who will keep my sister, Pankhuri, very happy. Trilok Ladla was all smiles to hold Pankhuri's hand. His mother was even happier knowing fully well his moist eyes' incident. Mrs Ladla pulling her son's legs – "Trilok, do you need a duster now?."

From joy to despair and now back to joy. What a fiasco!

The consent of Pankhuri's parents was essential and they were all too willing to come out of such a melee. The marriage would have made headlines had it been solemnized but they praised God for saving their skin from getting maligned.

41

EVERYTHING MUST COME TO AN END

Grey clouds formed in Shawn's eyes. Something ominous!

Shawn to himself - "Where is my mother? And what piece of paper she told me to keep in my pocket."

All these thoughts flowed like gurgling water in a river passing over polished pebbles and big and small boulders – only the audible sound was missing.

Shawn slipped into a remote corner, pulled out the piece of paper from his pocket to read.

Shawn and Mr Singh,

I, your step-mother, refuse to call you my son because I'm not fit to be your mother. What has happened was my brain-child to get a brother-sister married. I do not have the slightest remorse for it. It was my way of taking REVENGE – I'm spilling the beans today.

Over the pretense, I hated you when you were a child. You cried and your father, Mr Singh, would leave me alone to be with his son. I have been through an agonizing time with no chinks of hatred ever showing. It kept on accumulating till I became really hard-hearted. I cried inwardly but all my tears fell inside, never to show it's presence outside.

My hatred grew with age. I saw Mrs Jhunjhunwala was Pankhuri 's mother and the photograph of your dad's previous wife, which I found deep in his suit-case, was same. So, you were brother and sister, I understood.

Here was an opportunity to take revenge – to get a brother-sister married. I hate you and your father. He is the most selfish man who wanted only his own happiness and never thought what I wanted. Every girl`s dream is to be a real mother and go through the pangs of labour. He never wanted a child from me which he happily deprived me of. He just crushed my desires. How could I ever forgive him. I wanted to give him a scar that the world would spit on him. How do you like the jibe "Here goes the High and Mighty father who got his own son and daughter married- spit on him – "